Lieutenant Cameron RNVR

Lieutenant Cameron RNVR

Philip McCutchan

St. Martin's Press
New York

Library of Congress Cataloging in Publication Data

McCutchan, Philip, 1920–
  Lieutenant Cameron RNVR.

  1. World War, 1939-1945—Fiction. I. Title.
II. Title: Lieutenant Cameron R.N.V.R.
PR6063.A167L5   1985   823'.914   85-10902
ISBN 0-312-4 8 373-2

First published in Great Britain by Arthur Barker Ltd.

First U.S. Edition

10 9 8 7 6 5 4 3 2 1

1

LONDON in winter, London in wartime: early evening and a mist creeping up from the river to cross the Victoria Embankment and enshroud Whitehall Court and the Horse Guards. Austerity, a shortage of cigarettes once the duty-free supply brought on leave had run out, pubs that closed their doors once the beer was gone, whisky and gin very hard to come by, meals with a ceiling price of five bob but a fairly hefty cover charge allowed to the superior establishments patronized by officers on leave in the capital: dinner for two at the Ritz could cost three pounds, no less. Not much traffic, and taxis hard to find except usually at the main-line stations. Uniforms everywhere, and not only British. There were Poles, Czechs, Free French among others. No Americans yet, but they were bound to come, like the wail of the air raid sirens. Before long, the pavements of Piccadilly, like the sidewalks of New York, would be dappled with discarded, in-trodden chewing-gum....

Donald Cameron, leaving Queen Anne's Gate and the Second Sea Lord's department of the Admiralty, emerged into the mist as it stole through the London dark along Birdcage Walk and along St James's Park. Cameron shivered: it was colder than Aberdeen and that was saying something. Even his bridge coat didn't keep it out. He crossed into the park and walked fast for St James's Street where near the top he turned left into Blue Ball Yard. There was a small drinking club, called, appropriately, the Blue Ball Club. Officers only ... here, if you were lucky, you could get spirits. If you weren't, at least the bottled beer never seemed to run out. Cameron, who had become a member on his last leave, went in. The woman behind the bar didn't know him: he wasn't one of the Whitehall warriors, those with plenty of time for the London club scene.

'Member?' she asked.

He produced his membership card.

She asked, 'What's it to be, love?'

She was approaching her middle thirties, at a guess, and had a predatory smile. Cameron said, 'Whisky, please.'

'For you, love,' the woman said, 'it's a pleasure.' She delved down beneath the bar and came up with a bottle of John Haig, which was nectar. As she poured, she asked, 'Do I detect a slight Scotch accent?' She looked arch.

'Scots,' he corrected automatically. 'Yes. Thank you.' He took the glass, put a half-crown on the bar and collected his change. Drinking ashore was expensive: on board, you got a whisky for twopence. Cameron couldn't wait to be back at sea, and it wasn't just for the duty-free. London depressed him; it seemed to his eyes full of boozy majors in British Warms avoiding more active service. This he knew inside himself to be unfair but he couldn't help the surface thought. There were far too many from all three services who had sunk happily into cushy jobs and all the holders of staff appointments had become tarred with the same brush. London, air raids apart, was a parasite's dream. Within the next few minutes some of them came into the Blue Ball: brown jobs mostly, from the War Office, together with a commander RN who had a different look, as though his eyes were still gazing out over heaving waters and great distances and he wished to God they still were. For a moment those eyes lingered on Cameron and he read envy in them for someone too young to have a staff job. Then a leading Wren came in and Cameron got to his feet, glanced with raised eyebrows at the woman behind the bar and received a nod in return: Wren ratings who were also officers' girlfriends counted for club purposes as honorary officers themselves, on a temporary basis. Mary Anstey was acceptable.

Cameron took her in his arms and kissed her: in public, it was only a brief peck, but once again, the commander appeared envious. Mary sat down looking radiant and put a hand on the two wavy gold stripes on Cameron's cuff. 'Second stripe,' she said. 'You didn't say anything about that in your letters, Donald?'

He grinned. 'Only just got it ... a few days ago.'

'Accelerated promotion?'

'Something like that,' he said off-handedly. There was, he knew, more in the pipeline: the recommendation for a DSC had gone through and awaited the King's pleasure. He didn't want to talk about it; the past was still too painful, looming much larger than could be accounted for by mere memory. All the killings in Norway, the screams of men fearfully wounded, the noise of the Stukas that had come down to sink the old *Castle Bay*, the machine-gun bullets peppering the waters of the fjord, doing their best to finish off the survivors as the ship blew up. Then there was Jane, the girl from the Special Operations Executive ... her father, an admiral, had been quite largely responsible for that second stripe. Cameron appreciated it but felt undeserving, and a little sick at the thought that he'd got it as a result of so many other men dying. It was they who had been the heroes but you didn't promote the dead.

Mary, who had read between the lines of his letters, and had read the press reports too, seemed to understand and she didn't probe. But there was a pensiveness in her face and eyes: she knew he'd been for an interview with the minions of NA2SL – the Naval Assistant to the Second Sea Lord, the deity who allocated officers' appointments. Quietly she asked, as he lit her cigarette and her hair touched his bending cheek, 'What are they giving you, Donald?'

'First,' he said, 'leave. More leave, that is. Fourteen days.' He'd already had ten days, which he'd spent at home in Aberdeen. He felt he owed that to his parents, and in any case

7

Mary hadn't been available for more than a couple of evenings – she was working a watchkeeping system in Portsmouth and it was very demanding. Like a nurse, all she wanted to do when off duty was to catch up on her sleep.

'And after that?'

He lit his own cigarette and blew smoke into an already blue-hazed atmosphere. 'Cruiser,' he said.

'Which?'

He said solemnly, 'Don't forget the cartoons.' He thought of Hitler popping out from lavatory pans and under beds, ears flapping. 'Be Like Dad, Keep Mum.' He leaned across again and spoke into her ear. 'Not that it matters with you. The *Northumberland* ... one of the three-funnel County class jobs.'

Mary didn't probe further; in any case he couldn't have told her what the *Northumberland* was going to do, since he didn't know himself. The Lieutenant-Commander RNVR on duty in NA2SL's office hadn't been informative other than to advise Cameron to take white uniform with him. Mary said rather unsteadily, 'I wish you luck, Donald.' She hesitated, looking over his shoulder towards the group from the War Office and others who had drifted in. There was loud laughter as someone told a dirty story. Mary asked, 'Are you off back to Aberdeen?'

'Not tonight anyway. Tomorrow, perhaps. Unless there's an alternative.'

She said shyly, toying with her glass, 'I've got some unexpected leave. Ten days....'

Fifteen days later, with the Captain and Navigating Officer on the compass platform and the Chief Yeoman of Signals standing by on the flag deck with his telescope ready to read off any hoists from the Flag Officer in Charge, HMS *Northumberland* moved slowly through the fleet anchorage off the Tail o' the Bank in the Clyde. She moved for open water with special sea dutymen closed up and with her starboard bower anchor held on the brake at the waterline, ready to let go in an emergency.

As she came past an aircraft-carrier wearing a vice-admiral's flag, her Royal Marine bugler sounded the Still; the Captain saluted and all men on the upper deck froze for a moment until, as the flagship returned the salute, the Carry On sounded. Cameron, standing in the eyes of the ship with the Cable Officer, a lieutenant-commander RN, watched the great grey concourse of warships slide away astern. Aircraft-carriers, a battle-cruiser, two battleships, some twenty cruisers and destroyers plus other smaller craft. Since the outbreak of war in 1939, almost the whole Navy had left the southern dockyards of Portsmouth, Devonport and Chatham and had moved north for the Clyde and the Forth, for Londonderry and Scapa Flow. Greenock, away now to port as the *Northumberland* headed out for the anti-submarine boom, was a very naval town, complete with Wrennery, naval officers' club, and shore patrol to collect up drunks and ensure that ratings saluted all officers. The Scottishness had been largely submerged by gate-and-gaiters and by bull.

The cruiser passed through the boom and headed on for Toward Point and the Cumbraes; the wind grew stronger and keener, biting through duffel-coats and oilskins. There was a sea running already, even inside the Cumbraes; as the bow butted into the waves, spray was driven up, to blow across Cameron and the Cable Officer, back towards the eight-inch gun-turrets and the compass platform. It was cold and utterly dreary, the Clyde approaching its horrible worst in striking contrast to the days of sun and blue water that the area was also capable of. Soon after passing through the boom, past the gate vessel on station off Cloch Point, the Captain passed the orders to increase speed and secure the anchors for sea. The ship's company was sent to Cruising Stations, which meant a three-watch system – four on and eight off on the compass platform, at the guns and torpedo-tubes, in the engine-rooms and boiler-rooms, in the wheelhouse, and in the main transmitting and receiving rooms manned by the wireless telegraphists. Cameron was busy with the Cable Officer at the job of heaving the starboard anchor home to the hawse-pipe and securing the cables with Blake slips, bottle-screw slips, compressors and stoppers, when the *Northumberland* brought Toward Point abeam to starboard.

Inwards from Toward Point lay Rothesay, where the *Castle Bay* had sailed from. The memories flooded back but were best forgotten. As the cruiser made the Cumbraes and passed into the Firth with Arran looming huge on the starboard bow beyond Inchmarnock Water, Cameron found his memory shifting to that additional fourteen-day leave and the ten days he'd spent with Mary Anstey in a London hotel. That had been close to heaven, though it had left a vague feeling of guilt behind ... as Cameron made his way aft, the fo'c'sle now secured against the weather, a voice, raised in song, came up through a ventilator from one of the messdecks: '*I haven't said thanks for that lovely week-end, those few days in heaven you helped me to spend...*'

'Lieutenant Cameron, sir?'

Cameron turned; a seaman messenger was standing in his cabin doorway. 'That's me.'

'Captain's compliments, sir, and he'd like to see you on the compass platform.'

'Right, thank you.'

The man turned away; Cameron, who had been expecting the usual summons to meet the Captain ever since he had joined the ship the day before, took a brief look in his mirror and straightened his tie. Then he left his cabin and made his way along the alleyways and up a number of ladders to the compass platform, where the Captain was standing looking for'ard, his hands clasped behind a tall back that emphasized the gauntness of the figure. He seemed oblivious to everything but the disturbed seas ahead. Cameron waited. After a while he felt the need to make some announcement as to his presence; so he put a hand to his mouth and gave an embarrassed cough. Then the Captain spoke.

'If you're sick, report to the sick bay.'

'Sick, sir?'

10

'I dislike being coughed at.'

'Yes, sir. I'm sorry, sir.'

'If you wish to attract your Captain's attention upon some important matter, you use the words "Captain, sir". It's a time-honoured formula in His Majesty's Fleet.' The Captain turned. Captain Lees-Rimington was a four-ring Captain RN, a man with many years' experience of command. He looked the part: his was a formidable face, as cold and emotionless as Dartmoor granite. He said, 'You're Cameron, I take it.'

'Yes, sir. You sent for me, sir.'

'I'm aware of that. I had no time to send for you earlier.' Cold green eyes looked Cameron up and down, a sweeping, faintly hostile appraisal. 'Your last ship was the *Castle Bay*.'

Cameron was strongly tempted to say, 'I'm aware of that'; but refrained. He said, 'Yes, sir.'

'You'll find the *Northumberland* different. I run a taut ship, so does my Executive Officer. I'm told you did well aboard the *Castle Bay*, also in your previous appointment as a sub-lieutenant. I appreciate that – I'm glad to have you aboard.'

'Thank you, sir.'

'But let there be no swollen heads. Do you understand?'

Cameron felt himself flushing, felt the Captain's remark was unfair and uncalled-for; but all one could say to a Captain was 'yes, sir', and Cameron said it. Then he was dismissed with a curt nod and Captain Lees-Rimington turned his attention back to the waters ahead as the cruiser came abeam of Lamlash below the great eminence of Goat Fell.

Cameron went back to his cabin to prepare for the first dog watch on the compass platform, where he would be second Officer of the Watch under a lieutenant RN. This was a prospect he didn't care for; he had his watchkeeping certificate now, and was thus entitled to take charge of a watch on his own, but he had been slapped down already – in advance, as it were – and he was disinclined to put forward a claim that was clearly going to be acidly rejected. Perhaps it was all for the good of his soul, he thought philosophically. Nonetheless he wished himself back aboard the *Castle Bay*, or the *Wharfedale* in the Mediterranean, or even the *Carmarthen* in which he'd lurched about the North Atlantic during his lower-deck days as an ordinary seaman. Captain Lees-Rimington was his first experience – outside the stone frigates of his training days – of a four-ring Captain RN.

Cameron was on the compass platform again for the middle watch, the midnight to four a.m. By this time HMS *Northumberland* had passed through the North Channel and along the coastline of Northern Ireland, past Rathlin Island and Malin Head, and was well to the west of the Bloody Foreland off Donegal's north-western tip. The cruiser, well battened-down for bad weather, all deadlights closed, X and Y doors clamped shut, butted into the North Atlantic, making some westering before altering south to come down towards the Azores. It was a filthy night, with spray flinging over the gun-turrets and the compass platform, drenching those on watch before flying away aft along the upper deck. The cruiser had a nasty roll; the County class cruisers were vessels of very high freeboard and made unsteady gun platforms at the best of times. If they should meet the enemy tonight, Cameron thought, their shooting would be all over the show.

He peered ahead from the port wing through pitch darkness. That darkness seemed impenetrable, even to his binoculars. His eyes strained; he felt little more than an extra lookout in his subordinate position – that, and someone to run the routine of Rounds and the calling of the next watch. He could see nothing but the wild sea itself, the nearer waves that flattened out in spindrift. The gale battered at his ears through his balaclava. After a while he became aware of someone behind him, and he half turned. The Captain had come to the compass platform.

'There is something bearing red three-oh. Are you Cameron?'

'Yes, sir—'

'Why have you not reported, Cameron?' The voice was flat and cold.

12

'I've seen nothing, sir—'

'Then you are blind. There is a ship. Officer of the Watch?'

'Sir?' The RN lieutenant, by name Price, came across.

'An unknown ship to port – off the bow. Sound Action Stations.'

An iciness came to Cameron's guts as the rattlers sounded throughout the ship. He had already seen quite enough of action in the North Atlantic. The ship came alive with running men, seaboots pounding on the steel ladders as the guns' crews closed up and the directors were manned. To the Captain's order the turrets swung to bear on the port bow, and as they did so Cameron became aware at last of a shape, no more than a darker smudge against the dark sky, a smudge that rose and fell away again as the sea's action changed the juxtaposition of the two ships. If only they'd been fitted with radar, the new concept of the all-seeing eye ... but radar was far from universal yet and the anti-submarine escorts had priority.

The Captain said, 'Challenge.'

'Aye, aye, sir!' Price passed the order to the Chief Yeoman, who at once used his Aldis lamp to make the identification signal for the day. The response was immediate. A flash appeared on the port bow, a brilliant flash of orange that split the night, and a whistling sound was heard overhead. As the Captain ordered the *Northumberland*'s main armament to open, the eight-inch turrets for'ard of the compass platform erupted in balls of flame and an ear-splitting roar.

2

THE night became like day, in patches, as the guns belched flame. More shells came across the *Northumberland*'s decks, but flew harmlessly over and into the boiling sea. The enemy ship's gunnery was unusually poor, and Lees-Rimington was handling his ship well, standing like a gaunt statue in the fore part of the compass platform and passing his helm orders back to the Officer of the Watch at the binnacle.

Then the *Northumberland*'s guns scored a hit: two shells, it seemed, from one of the fore turrets, twin guns causing twin explosions on their shadowy target. Brilliance shot from each end of the vessel, and in the sudden flame the Chief Yeoman of Signals saw the ensign.

He called out, 'She's a Frog, sir! Vichy French ... not German, sir!'

The Captain turned his head slightly. 'Perhaps that explains the poor gunnery.'

'Shall we cease firing, sir?' the Officer of the Watch asked.

'No. They're the enemy as much as the Germans now.' Lees-Rimington brought up his binoculars. He was in time to see the end. More shells exploded aboard the Frenchman, which was a destroyer. Then a gigantic explosion came; a shell had most probably found a magazine. Lees-Rimington ordered a searchlight put on the scene. As the light beamed out and steadied, there were more explosions. Debris flew into the air; the destroyer had broken in half, and for a brief moment the two ends stood clearly in view, thrusting from the sea until they went down fast, independently, and van-

14

ished below the racing waves to leave men struggling in the water.

Lees-Rimington lowered his glasses. 'Off searchlight,' he said. 'Course, two-seven-oh degrees. Maximum revolutions. I shall not start the zig-zag. U-boats won't surface in this weather.'

'Survivors, sir?'

'I do not propose to stop for survivors,' Lees-Rimington said coldly. 'There may be other enemy vessels in the vicinity. The ship will remain at first degree of readiness until further orders.'

Under the full power of her screws, the *Northumberland* raced on into the night.

There was plenty of comment. Amongst the ship's company some were for the skipper, many against. The argument was still going on next morning, when the *Northumberland* had reduced to cruising stations and had altered to the south, still shouldering through heavy seas beneath a desolate overcast. The Chief Gunner's Mate had been at Oran the year before; though he hadn't been long in the *Northumberland*, the facts of his last-but-one appointment were already very well known to his messmates. Now, when he said, 'I was with Somerville,' the Chief Petty Officer Telegraphist rolled his eyes to the deckhead, lit a fag and made certain suggestions as to what he could do with Admiral Somerville.

'Now look here—'

The CPO Telegraphist lifted a hand. 'All right, all right – sorry! Nothing wrong with Somerville, except anyone'd think he'd come aboard with you.' He got to his feet and left the mess, having heard it all before. Sod the French, the Vichy lot that was, they'd asked for it, though sure enough it was bloody hard to steam off and leave them to it when not so long ago they'd been their gallant allies. Oran had been a rotten job for those that had had to do it.

After the CPO Telegraphist had gone, the Chief Gunner's Mate sat and brooded on Oran. At the French naval base of

Mers-el-Kebir, near Oran, there had been the *Dunkerque* and the *Strasbourg*, both of them battle-cruisers, a couple of battleships – *Bretagne* and *Provence* – together with half-a-dozen destroyers and a seaplane carrier. Vice-Admiral Sir James Somerville, flying his flag in the battle-cruiser *Hood* and commanding the newly-formed Force H based on Gibraltar, had been ordered to close Oran with the battleships *Resolution* and *Valiant* plus the *Ark Royal*, *Arethusa*, *Enterprize* and a number of destroyers. When each of the alternatives Somerville was authorized to put to the French admiral had been rejected, the French fleet showed signs of clearing for action; and at 1745 on 3 July Admiral Somerville had opened fire with his massive array of guns . . .

The Chief Gunner's Mate wiped his face with a handkerchief. The Frogs had been *kaput*. It had been very, very nasty and there had been a heavy loss of life. At the time of the 1937 Fleet review at Spithead, the Chief Gunner's Mate, then a leading seaman in the *Rodney*, had hob-nobbed happily ashore with French *matelots* from the representative ship of the French Navy, the *Dunkerque*, all set to watch His Majesty King George VI steam down the review lines in the royal yacht *Victoria and Albert*. To him, the French had seemed the best of the mixed bunch of sailors attending the review: better than the Germans and the Eyeties, even then obviously ready to become the enemy . . . and as for the Russians, who called their admiral a flagman, well, God preserve him from *that* lot. He had drunk with the French in quite a few of Pompey's proliferating pubs and he'd learned the words of the 'Marseillaise' and taught the Frogs 'God Save The King'. When drunk enough, they'd linked arms and bawled the words out all along Commercial Road and Edinburgh Road and down Queen Street to the main gate of the dockyard. Even the coppers had turned a blind eye; the police didn't interfere too much with the Navy, and anyway it had been a festive week.

Maybe his guns had killed a lot of old friends at Oran; last night, too. The skipper might be right and he might be wrong; but two facts remained: the destroyer certainly hadn't flashed her identification following the *Northumberland*'s challenge; and Lees-Rimington was a hard man in any situation, as hard and inflexible as cast iron.

During the forenoon, the Captain spoke to his ship's company over the tannoy.

He said crisply, coldly, 'This is your Captain speaking. My guns' crews did well last night. The enemy, as you all know, was destroyed.' He paused. 'But not soon enough to prevent her sending out a situation report to the German Naval command at Brest. Our position at that time will now be known to the Germans, who will make their own assessments. From now on, I must consider the ship marked. Nevertheless, I intend to proceed in execution of my orders, which are to intercept and sink any enemy commerce raiders that I find in the South Atlantic or the Indian Ocean beyond the range of the U-boats. That is all.'

He switched off and turned away, stalking to the fore part of the compass platform where for a minute or so he stared out at the thrashing seas, eyes hard beneath the gold-oak-leaved peak of his cap. Somewhere ahead of his course – perhaps very far ahead, as far as the waters to east or west of the Cape of Good Hope – lay, to the best of the Admiralty's knowledge, certain vessels of the German Navy intent upon destroying such British ships as still sailed independently of convoy, or even the convoys themselves. The cruisers *Emden* and *Leipzig*, the pocket-battleship *Admiral Scheer* and a number of armed merchantmen were at large; though the teeth of the German commerce raiders had by this stage of the war been to some extent drawn, the menace was lurking still. Captain Lees-Rimington squared his shoulders. His ship would give a good account of herself, and never mind the gnawing anxiety that was always with him: the *Northumberland*'s high freeboard and her thin, unarmoured sides that would no more keep out a properly aimed shell than a wooden door would keep out the teeth of a determined rat.

The Captain turned to the Officer of the Watch. 'I shall

be in my sea-cabin. Call me in accordance with standing orders.'

'Aye, aye, sir.'

The *Northumberland* steamed on, rolling heavily, her decks and superstructure wet with spray, the White Ensign straining from the gaff and the Captain's commissioning pennant as stiff as an arrow at the mainmast head. The damp overcast brought an air of depression to the compass platform. The Officer of the Watch, an RNR lieutenant, had seen it all before, having spent some years running to South America. Familiar waters, but nonetheless dreary today. The depression lifted a little when the bridge messenger came up with cocoa.

They all knew, now, where they were going and what they were going to do. It wasn't reassuring. The old *Northumberland* had never been designed for the job she'd been given; she was going to be very exposed and vulnerable. But the Navy was desperately short of ships and everything had to be thrown into the battle to keep Britain fed and supplied with arms and ammunition and oil fuel, those things that were under threat from the surface raiders and the U-boats. The ship's company talked about it in the broadside messes, in the warrant officers' mess, in the gunroom and in the wardroom. Not so much in the latter; most of the officers had known already what the orders were.

Lunch that day was the usual wardroom meal: nondescript soup, two slices of beef with potatoes, watery cabbage and some sad-looking carrots out of a tin, all submerged in thin gravy; rice pudding, and finally cheese. Mousetrap, with a hard skin. Cameron was seated alongside another RNVR lieutenant, named Canning; he was gradually meeting his new shipmates.

Canning poked at the cheese with a knife and said, 'Paymaster's being stingy again. Lining his coffers to spend on the wife and kids.' He glanced at Cameron, sitting beside him. 'You married?' he asked.

'No. Are you?'

Canning nodded. 'Yes. Just before the war. A happy little nest down in Cornwall. Bodmin. Bugger Hitler.'

'What were you doing?'

'Working in a bank. I didn't like it much, but I don't like this at all.' Canning deserted the cheese and instead reached out for an apple from a dish. He started peeling it. In a low voice he started singing: *'When this bloody war is over, oh how happy we will be ... no more—'*

There was an interruption from the head of the table: the Commander. 'Stop that damn singing! It's not done. There's a time and a place.'

Canning said, 'Sorry, sir, I didn't think you could hear.' He turned to Cameron and whispered, 'Starchy bugger is our Commander. Look at his shirt.' Cameron looked: the cuffs were stiffly starched, making the three gold rings lie flat and smooth above. 'Pre-war in all things,' Canning said. 'Dyed-in-the-wool RN. What were you, pre-war?'

Cameron told him. 'I was going to join my father's trawler firm. I'd have gone to sea first—'

'To sea? Well, sooner you than me. I don't know why I didn't join the army, except that I don't fancy trenches either. Roll on my twelve, as the lower-deck chappies say.' Canning looked at his watch. 'I'm going to get some sleep – I've got the first dog in the director.'

'You're gunnery, are you?' Cameron asked.

'For my sins, yes. I had an eye to comfort. It's better protected from the wind in the director.'

Canning went off; Cameron sat on over a cup of coffee. Big ships ... they were very different from destroyers, even more different from the *Castle Bay*. Plenty of bull, bags of gold braid, and a feeling that dress and deference were more important than the ship's fighting capacity. Cameron's reading had told him that in fact, in the later years of Queen Victoria's Navy, a warship's appearance had in many cases been considered of much greater importance than efficiency. Watertight doors and cables had been burnished, guns had not been fired in case the paintwork should be spoiled ... that

19

was a long time ago now, and times had changed; but Cameron felt himself more at one with the small ships where, though life was hard and uncomfortable, the comradeship was enough to compensate and there was a strong feeling of all hands pulling together, of a total interdependence. He was already aware that the *Northumberland* was divided into three main, almost watertight, compartments: the Executive Branch, the Engine-room, and the Accountant Branch, with the doctors and padre on a kind of roving commission, able to circulate freely. It was a kind of mutual suspicion between branches, not very overt, but there all the same. It would disappear in action or emergency; but in point of fact very little of a big ship's time was spent in action and in between there was an immensity of boredom. Cameron looked over the rim of his coffee cup; he had come down for lunch late, and now all the others had left the table and had taken up positions of comfort in the wardroom chairs and settees. The Paymaster Commander was lying back almost parallel with the deck, legs thrust out, reading a two-day-old newspaper; the Commander (E) was similarly stretched out with his eyes closed. The PMO, a surgeon lieutenant-commander, was sipping a brandy and yarning to his Number Two, a surgeon lieutenant. A paymaster lieutenant was asleep and snoring; two watchkeeping lieutenants were playing shove-ha'penny over by the starboard door leading into the after lobby, neither of them looking very interested. The Gunnery Officer, a lieutenant-commander RN, was sitting on the leather-topped fireplace surround pulling at his luxuriant beard and staring into space. Wardroom servants were clearing up the remains of lunch; Cameron left them all to it and made his way to his cabin in the after flat where, right in the stern, a Royal Marine sentry with a rifle mounted guard over the currently empty quarters of Captain Lees-Rimington. In the racks nearby, the rifles clanked against the retaining chain running through the trigger-guards, moving to the roll of the ship as she surged through the filthy weather. There was a nasty damp fug below, and no fresh air.

Cameron turned in. Aboard a cruiser at sea, when one was off watch and had no other pressing duties to perform, an afternoon nap was the order of the day.

Inside the German Naval Command building in Brest, the map counters were being moved as the hour-by-hour position of the British cruiser was plotted, starting from the information signalled by the French destroyer when action had opened: Captain Lees-Rimington's worst fears were being confirmed.

A rear-admiral of the Imperial German Navy, a thick-set man with a trim, jutting beard, crystallized his thoughts aloud, using a pointer to illustrate them.

'Down here, by the Falklands, a British merchant ship, carrying refrigerated meat, from Australia. Here, a British convoy from Cape Town to Freetown in Sierra Leone, thence for the Clyde. Here, between the Falklands and the Azores, two of our raiders. And somewhere here, the *Northumberland*. Lartner?'

A lieutenant stiffened to attention. '*Ja, Herr Admiral?*'

The Rear-Admiral tapped his pointer on the *Northumberland*'s estimated position. 'We are making the assumption the British cruiser is heading south.'

'*Ja, Herr Admiral.*'

'We do not want her interfering with our raiders, Lartner. Find out if the *Oberhausen* is ready for sea yet. If she is, I have orders for her. She is to proceed at once in pursuit of the *Northumberland*, which is to be sunk without delay.'

'*Ja, Herr Admiral.*'

Lieutenant Lartner clicked his heels once again and went to a telephone. The heavy cruiser *Oberhausen* was now reported as being at four hours' notice for sea; and the orders for her Captain were passed. Four hours later the German ship had steam and was proceeding outwards past Cameret-sur-Mer to cross the Bay of Biscay into the Atlantic, her great guns trained to the fore-and-aft line, with their tompions in place against the heavy seas, but ready to clear for action to the glory of the Third Reich. Her Captain strutted his bridge, up and down; there was much honour to be gained from the single-handed sinking of a British cruiser. Once the *Oberhausen* was clear of the inshore waters, speed was increased to the maximum. The position of the *Northumberland* was largely a matter of guesswork, but guesses could be intelligently made and the operational control at Brest would indicate immediately by wireless when further information came to hand, possibly as a result of sightings by the Luftwaffe.

That evening, a little before the ship went to dusk action stations, the Captain did what many commanding officers would have done earlier: he sent for Lieutenants Price and Cameron to administer a rebuke for their failure to spot the Vichy destroyer before he himself had done so. Captain Lees-Rimington believed that to let an officer or man stew for a while added to the effect of the dressing-down when at last it came. Price and Cameron waited upon the Captain in his sea-cabin. Price went in first; he emerged with a set expression and avoided Cameron's eye: the RN didn't like being taken down a peg along with the RNVR.

Cameron was next. He knocked and entered the sea-cabin. The Captain was seated at a small knee-hole desk, dealing with some of the inevitable paperwork that had to be attended to at sea and in harbour.

He swivelled to face Cameron; staring him up and down he said, 'You know why you're here, I take it?'

'Yes, sir.'

'If you have an excuse, make it.'

Cameron swallowed and said, 'No excuse, sir.'

'I see. You admit dereliction of your duty?'

'Yes, sir. I'm sorry, sir.'

'Well may you be sorry,' Lees-Rimington said in a hard voice. 'By your action, or lack of it rather, you hazarded my ship and all her company. Lack of extreme vigilance at sea causes deaths. You realize that?'

22

'Yes, sir.'

'You may say, the bridge lookout on the port side should have seen the ship. So he should, and he will be placed in the Commander's report. But that does not excuse an officer his own duty. Do you agree?'

'Yes, sir.'

The Captain was silent for a few moments, staring Cameron straight in the eyes meanwhile. His own eyes were those so often found in naval officers of his generation: cold, not exactly arrogant, but supercilious and devoid of feeling, the kind of look that said the person stared at was scarcely human, was of no account at all. Still staring, he spoke at last. 'Your name will be entered in the log,' he said. 'You will initial the entry when the Navigating Officer has written up the fair copy. You may go.'

'Thank you, sir.' Cameron, his face red, turned about and left the sea-cabin. He felt a sense of unfairness, felt that the Captain had shown inconsistency: if the seaman lookout's failure was blamed upon the second Officer of the Watch, then that officer's failure should be blamed upon the senior OOW, the person ultimately responsible ... yet there was in fact a consistency insofar as they were all being punished together, for no doubt Price would be logged too. And Cameron didn't attempt to hide from himself that he had been at fault; if the Captain had been able to see the vague shadow in the night, then so should he have done. No use crying over spilt milk, no use sulking. There was no room for sulkers at sea: he just had to keep his eyes skinned in future and hope the logging wouldn't have too adverse an effect on his future while the war lasted.

In the sea-cabin, when Cameron had left, the Captain slowly swivelled his chair towards the desk. He stared at the blankness of the bulkhead behind the desk, almost unseeingly. He shifted a little in his chair, feeling nagging pain: damned indigestion again! Those two youngsters ... the logging might go a little way against Price in his career, but Cameron would hardly notice it as an RNVR with no naval future to worry about. Cameron hadn't made any attempt at self-justification and that was much in his favour, but he'd had to be dealt with in the same manner as Price, who had been surly. The whole thing was unforgivable: the ship had been endangered navigationally as well as in the line of action. Loggings ... Captain Lees-Rimington's thoughts went back over the years, over many oceans, many ships, many landfalls in a long career. He had entered the Navy via the RN College at Osborne only three years after Queen Victoria had died; his training as a naval cadet had been long and hard. Those had been the days of an iron discipline and free use of the cane, the days when the Captain had been very God and the Commander just a shade less so. Naval cadets were rendered speechless before the majesty of the Captain and the Commander, and they stood in awe of their Term Lieutenants as well. And they'd had to shine, they'd had to be damned good at boat-work, at knots and splices, at navigation and gunnery and seamanship, and they had to attend to their class-room work too. By the time they became midshipmen they had changed from children to men; as midshipmen in the battleships and cruisers of the British Fleet they'd had to take charge of the steam picquet-boats with their hardy, seasoned crews, who did not always take kindly to being under the orders of youngsters who could have been their sons, but who respected the rigorous training that produced midshipmen. That was the way to begin learning the exercise of command and responsibility – in Lees-Rimington's view, the only way. Now the breed was being thinned out: Price, for instance, had joined by the process known as Special Entry – he'd not been to Dartmouth which had finally replaced Osborne but had joined at the age of seventeen and trained aboard the former monitor *Erebus* in Portsmouth harbour and in the training cruiser *Frobisher*. He had missed the long cadet years from the age of thirteen and a half. It wasn't quite the same. Command was not quite so inbred, not so deeply instilled. And then there was the RNVR: keen but inexperienced in the ways of the Navy and of the sea itself.

Lees-Rimington shifted again, cursing his stomach and the bile that rose like the puking of a seasick boy. The doctor had spoken of ulcers, but that was rubbish, nothing wrong that bismuth couldn't cure in the end. RNVR ... no, a logging wouldn't do any harm. The Captain went back into the past again. In the first decade of the century and the years leading up to the Great War he had served as midshipman and then as sub-lieutenant aboard the battleships *Dreadnought*, *King Edward VII* and *Hindustan*, and aboard the cruisers *Cressy* and *Powerful*. In August 1914 he had been a junior lieutenant aboard the battle-cruiser *Lion* when the ships of the British Fleet had steamed away from Spithead, past his Majesty the King aboard the royal yacht, fading into a sea mist to their war stations, the mightiest gathering of warships that the world had ever seen. Logging? Lees-Rimington smiled with a touch of wistfulness. He could see it now, in the careful handwriting of the fair log, signed by his Captain and initialled by himself: 'Had occasion this day to reprimand Lieutenant Hubert Guy Sutherland Lees-Rimington, Royal Navy, in that he did fail to pay the proper respects as Officer of the Watch in harbour when passed by a steam pinnace aboard which the Commander-in-Chief, Portsmouth, was embarked.' It wasn't a very dreadful crime when viewed in retrospect, but Captain Lees-Rimington believed that it could have had something to do with the fact that he was nearing the top of the Captains' List while many junior to him were gaining promotion to Flag rank, those who had never been logged at all. It could have been a factor causing him to have missed the boat in an overcrowded race in which those with any blemishes were automatically discarded. A logging was a logging to a career officer, and never mind that it had been given by a bad-tempered, autocratic Captain in a particularly foul mood following upon an acid signal from the affronted Commander-in-Chief....

The Captain turned as a knock came at the sea-cabin door and the Midshipman of the Watch entered.

'Captain, sir—'

'Yes, what is it?'

'Permission to go to dusk action stations, sir, please.'

Lees-Rimington nodded. 'Yes.' He glanced at his watch and took up his cap. As the midshipman left, he pulled on his duffel-coat and followed the youngster to the compass platform, where he acknowledged the salute of the Officer of the Watch and moved to the fore part. He stared down at the seas washing over the fo'c'sle and around the eight-inch gunturrets. The light was fading as the bugle, sounding over the tannoy, sent the ship's company to action stations, a routine measure at dusk and dawn, the times when the enemy liked to attack, the traditional times of slow reactions and responses. Lees-Rimington raised his head and sniffed the wind: it was blowing strongly from the north-east, slap on his port quarter. It was going to be a dirty night, not one on which to have to engage in action. The ship was rolling viciously; it would be virtually impossible to train and lay the main armament. The Admiralty constructors and naval architects should have thought about war when the County class cruisers were designed! They had been chiefly laid down for the peacetime purpose of showing the flag around the Empire. Comfortably equipped, plenty of head-room below, spacious messdecks for the ratings, but abominable when it came to gunnery. Lees-Rimington listened to the sound of the wind; he had a feeling it was going to increase.

'Captain, sir.'

'Yes?' Lees-Rimington turned to face a paymaster lieutenant.

'Cypher from the Admiralty, sir, prefix Most Immediate.'

'What does it say? No – wait. Bring it across to the chart table.'

'Aye, aye, sir.' The Paymaster Lieutenant followed the Captain to the after part of the compass platform. Lees-Rimington ducked his head below the painted canvas screen and switched on the light. The signal, broken down into plain language, was placed before him. He read: NORTHUMBERLAND FROM ADMIRALTY, RECONNAISSANCE AIRCRAFT

REPORT HEAVY CRUISER OBERHAUSEN LEFT BREST MAKING SOUTH-WEST ACROSS BISCAY.

Lees-Rimington backed away from the chart table, temporarily blinded by the light. He informed the Officer of the Watch and the Navigating Officer of the contents of the cypher. He said, 'Note the addressee.'

'Sir?'

Lees-Rimington said irritably, 'Just us, Pilot. Just us! Not repeated to C-in-C Home Fleet, or Western Approaches. That means no one else is being ordered to intercept – that's how I read it. We're on our own, sink or swim.'

'We'll be a needle in a haystack, sir.'

'Yes, I know. If we meet ... what main armament does the *Oberhausen* carry?'

The Navigating Officer said, 'Same as us, sir – eight eight-inch.'

'But she's armoured. We're not. We'll have to hope to miss her. But if we meet her, we fight.' Lees-Rimington moved back to the fore part of the compass platform and lowered his tall frame into the seat provided for the Captain's use on the starboard side. He might have to make a night of it: it had to be the *Northumberland* that got the first salvo in. His stomach seemed to be on fire and there was a foul taste in his mouth. He said, 'Send down to the PMO. I want some bismuth.'

'Are you sick, sir?'

'No. Just do as I say, that's all.' The gale was stiffening now, as he had thought it would. Lees-Rimington shivered beneath the thick duffel-coat. It was as cold as ice and a moment later the snow started.

3

As a precaution, action stations were not fallen out but were maintained indefinitely on the Captain's order. The buzz went through the ship in no time at all: the Jerries had left Brest to get them. The buzz exaggerated, as all buzzes did: their position was known to the German naval command and they were being overtaken by a pocket-battleship. This misconception didn't last long. Lees-Rimington, who knew all about buzzes and the galley wireless, gave his ship's company the facts over the tannoy. They most probably wouldn't be found, but if they were they would give as good as they got.

'And hooray for Merry England,' a stout three-badge able seaman said in the after shell-handling room as the Captain's voice ceased in the flat above. The handling-room hadn't yet been battened-down beneath its hatch, but it would be when the guns opened, and the AB and his mates with it. 'We're all going to be bloody 'eroes, that's what. If I was the skipper, I'd beat it 'ome to the Clyde, stuff me if I wouldn't.'

There was a laugh. 'Who'd want to stuff you, Stripey?'

Stripey Barnard took a swipe at the speaker, an ordinary seaman of little more than eighteen years of age. 'Speak to your seniors when they speaks to you, Lofty, otherwise shut up, all right?'

'Skipper knows what he's doing,' the youth said. 'We joined to fight ... or didn't we?'

'No, we didn't,' the AB said viciously, 'not in this tub, anyway. You only got to *look* at her bloody side to make an

28

'ole and I got a missus an' kids down in Guz – and I don't reckon to die so Lees-Rimington can bask in glory in the next world, sod me—'

'Put a sock in it,' a voice said from above. Stripey, so called on account of his three good-conduct badges – twelve years' undetected crime, it was said – had a foghorn in his throat and it had carried up the shaft to the flat. A petty officer was looking down. 'Any more o' that and you go in the rattle.'

The fat man gave a mock salute. 'Sorry I'm sure,' he said in a mincing tone, but kept it low this time. Any road, he'd said his piece and he had no choice never mind what. He made the best of the comparative comfort of the handling-room, which was a sight better than being on the upper deck as the *Northumberland* ran before the mounting gale. All that spray ... Stripey slid to the deck and rolled into a corner and closed his eyes. Might as well get some kip. With luck, he'd be finished off in his sleep and never know what had hit him till he emerged in heaven and found the skipper there waiting to be saluted. Just before slipping into sleep he had a nightmare thought: if you all went down, or up, in the same ship together, then maybe you remained in the bloody Andrew for all eternity, still under the thumb of the wardroom nobs and forever attending Divisions, and Defaulters, and Quarters Clean Guns, and Divine Service....

Medicine was taken to the compass platform by the PMO in person. It wasn't bismuth, but Lees-Rimington didn't argue about it. Dr Peterson knew very well that the Captain was inclined to call everything bismuth that went into his stomach by way of medication. The PMO also knew that the Captain was developing a stomach ulcer but it was no use stressing the diagnosis again since it was rejected each time it was advanced. The PMO, who was RNVR – a fact for which the whole ship's company piously thanked God, since RN medical officers were supposed to be able to diagnose only VD and to treat everything else with Black Draught – had found himself stumped by Lees-Rimington, who had virtually ordered his own diagnosis: plain indigestion, nothing more. Well, it was his funeral and nothing to be done about it, at any rate until they got back from this operation; then the Captain might be persuaded to have a check-up in the base hospital ashore.

Lees-Rimington handed back the glass. 'Tastes filthy,' he said.

'The worse it tastes, the more good it does you, sir.'

'That's doctors' jargon.'

'I dare day.' The PMO grinned. 'Are you going to stay up here all night, sir?'

'Yes, if necessary. Are you all ready for action if it comes, PMO?'

'Yes, sir. Sick bay, emergency dressing stations—'

'Good. I believe you've not been in action before?'

'No, I haven't—'

'Then you won't be acquainted with gunshot wounds. Pity. It won't be quite like dealing with old ladies' piles, but I'm sure you'll do your best.'

The PMO said, 'I'll be trying, sir.'

'What did you say?' Lees-Rimington's voice was harshly angry. 'No, don't repeat it, please. I don't like officers who tell me they'll try. You must succeed – not simply try. Many lives will be dependent upon you and your staff.'

The Captain turned away dismissingly. The PMO went down the ladder to the upper deck and through the screen into the superstructure, glad to be out of the wind and spray. The Captain's reference to old ladies' piles rankled a little: in civilian life Dr Peterson had been at St Thomas's doing hospital time on a children's ward prior to putting up his own plate. It had been the proximity of the Thames and the London Division RNVR's drill-ship, HMS *President*, that had led him to become a peacetime 'Saturday-afternoon sailor' as the Wavy Navy's personnel had been dubbed. It was to that peacetime entry and his resultant seniority over the wartime entrants that he owed his recent extra half stripe as a surgeon lieutenant-commander, so the effort had been worth while.

30

But now he found himself wondering how he would make out if action came. Never before had he been the senior doctor available: in hospital there had always been a consultant somewhere around. Now it would all be up to him. Medical knowledge was one thing and he didn't for a moment doubt his professional capacity; but the application of knowledge in a literally explosive situation, with the ship possibly on fire and fractured steel bulkheads twisted around the screaming bodies, was a different thing. His staff, which in normal routine seemed over large, was in fact small enough: a surgeon lieutenant, a CPO sick berth attendant, two leading sick berth attendants and four ordinary SBAs. Plus the unofficial help of the chaplain when he wasn't required to minister to the dying.

Peterson went to his action station in the sick bay. He sat for a moment making a further mental check that all medical action requirements had been complied with, then got up and went over to a cot containing his one bed patient – so far. This was a young ordinary seaman who had hurt his head and back falling down a ladder in a seaway just after leaving the Clyde.

'All right, Jones?' he asked.

'Yes, sir.'

'Comfortable?'

'Yes, thank you, sir.' Worried eyes looked back at the PMO. 'The ship's still at action stations, sir.'

'Yes. Nothing to worry about.'

'I'm not worried about that, sir. Not really, like.'

The PMO nodded, looking shrewdly at the young face that as yet scarcely needed to be shaved. Something was going on in the lad's mind and Peterson wanted to help. He said quietly, 'Tell me what the trouble is. Get it off your chest. I've all the time in the world.'

'Yes, sir. Thank you, sir. It's . . . well, sir, I got the buzz from an SBA that the Jerries have come out from Brest looking for us and they know where we are—'

'I doubt that bit, Jones. I doubt it very strongly.'

'Yes, sir. I'm not worried about meself, sir, not really, it's me mum, see.'

Peterson nodded. 'Where is she, Jones?'

'London, sir, Hackney. Them bloody bombers.'

'She'll be all right. Try not to worry. Everyone goes down to the shelters. Don't tell me your mother doesn't.'

'No, sir, but it's ... well, she's all on her own, sir. Me dad was killed at Dunkirk, in a destroyer. Both me brothers went down in the *Royal Oak*. There's no one else left, only me.'

Peterson understood well enough and wished he was better equipped to cope. He put a hand on the youth's shoulder and said, 'A naval family. Something to be very proud of. I'm sure your mother is.' Then he turned away. This wasn't a doctor's job, it was the padre's really. The padre was a good man, one who could talk without unction about God and the after life and reunions in a better place. But even that would be unlikely to help much when a young lad saw his mother left without any support at all in a world at war. The PMO's fingernails dug hard into his palms: God damn Hitler.

On the compass platform the Navigating Officer approached the Captain. 'Captain, sir?'

'What is it, Pilot?'

'I think we might do better to alter westwards for a while, sir.'

'Your reason?'

'Confuse the enemy, sir.'

Lees-Rimington stirred impatiently. 'Rubbish. We could be here, there, or anywhere. It's in the hands of chance. Sheer chance.'

'But—'

'We hold our course and speed. There's no more to be said.'

The Navigating Officer shrugged and turned away. Talk about rigidity: Lees-Rimington was about as flexible as a coffin. In the faint glow of light from the binnacle the Navigator caught the eye of the Officer of the Watch, Lieutenant Price. A wink was exchanged behind the Captain's back. Price was bending sideways to murmur something in the Navigator's ear when the *Northumberland* took an exceptionally heavy sea on her quarter and gave a sudden heaving lurch that took Price totally unawares and unready. He grabbed at the binnacle for support, missed, slipped on the wet deck, somehow or other got his legs twisted, and went flat, catching his head on the binnacle as he fell. He gave a shout of pain.

Lees-Rimington said, 'What was that?'

'Price, sir,' the Navigating Officer answered. 'I think he's broken his leg.'

'How unseamanlike. Send down to the sick bay, a Neil Robinson stretcher for my action Officer of the Watch, who has broken his leg on the compass platform.' Lees-Rimington's acid voice made it sound an utterly impossible thing for a sane man and a seaman to do. 'Cameron?'

Cameron answered from the port wing. 'Sir?'

'Take over the watch.'

'Aye, aye, sir!' Cameron moved to the binnacle and made the routine report on taking over. 'Course, one-eight-four degrees, sir, maximum revolutions, telegraphs at full ahead all engines.'

'Very good. Don't slide about like an eel.'

'No, sir.'

He had his chance now; he was going to make the most of it and not incur the Captain's strictures in any way whatsoever. It was like the lead part falling to the understudy as a result of misfortune. A party of seamen under the Surgeon Lieutenant and the LSBA was quickly on the compass platform with a Neil Robinson stretcher, an affair like a strait-jacket into which Price was strapped and lowered down the ladder. The Surgeon Lieutenant had confirmed the broken leg diagnosis; Lees-Rimington made no comment; he had already said all he had to say.

The *Northumberland* steamed on fast, still running with the gale on her port quarter, rising and falling to the seas that swept beneath her bottom plating, the spray flinging furiously

33

across the decks and the guns, drenching the Chief Gunner's Mate as he made his way around the turrets and the ack-ack and close- range weapons, checking, criticizing, praising, ever watchful and jealous for his department's instant readiness at all times, though he didn't see much point in so much readiness tonight. Second degree would have been enough, maybe more than enough. The Jerries were very likely no closer to spotting them than they were any other ships at sea all over the world, and all perishing ships didn't stay closed up at action stations the whole bleeding time, oh no! The Chief Gunner's Mate didn't go much on the business of watch on, stop on. The skipper was too careful by half; the ship would go to action stations in a flash when necessary. The old *Northumberland* had a first-rate ship's company, not many slackers and the Chief Gunner's Mate, knowing precisely who those slackers were, would be on hand to put the fear of God into their hearts and his own boot into their backsides when the alarm rattlers went. Moving through the superstructure, where it was nice and dry, on his way to the after turrets after checking through the fore part of the ship, the CGM encountered the Master-at-Arms, who at action stations had a roving commission to ensure tight discipline. He stopped for a word with the ship's chief of police. 'Still at the bull, then, Master?'

MAA Pond grinned back at him. 'If it wasn't for you an' me, Jim, we'd never get to bloody sea at all, right?'

'Right. Heard about Price?'

'No, what?'

'Slid on his arse,' the CGM said briefly. 'Hors de bloody combat, he is. We're in the hands of the Wavy Navy, now.'

'Gawd strewth,' the MAA said solemnly. 'Which one, may I ask?'

'Cameron, one that just joined. Unknown quantity. Some's good, some's not.'

'Ah, well,' the MAA said soothingly, 'Skipper an' Navvy's up there an' all. Can't come to much harm, can we? What d'you make the chances of meeting up with this *Oberhausen*, eh?'

'Bloody little.'

'You hope!'

'Speak for yourself, Master.' The CGM spat on his hands. 'I just want to see what my guns can do. That's what we're here for, all of us. Guns is the whole bloody point. No guns, no ship.'

'Get away with you,' MAA Pond said jeeringly. 'You're full of bull like all gunner's mates, proper bloody Whale Island, all you do is bugger up the paintwork and make a bloody great racket over my cabin when I'm trying to kip in the afternoon watch.' He proceeded on his way, accompanied by the inevitable torch that had replaced the candle-lantern used in former times. The CGM heard him going flap-flap along the deck: MAA Pond had big feet, as all members of the Regulating Branch were popularly supposed to have. The Regulating Petty Officers were known as crushers on account of the number of cockroaches slaughtered by their boots during their nocturnal prowls.

A grim grey dawn came up to lighten the sky just a little, to reveal the white-capped, spindrift-covered waves stretching as far as the eye could see in all directions. It was a lonely feeling. Cruisers seldom steamed without a destroyer escort, but destroyers could not be spared for the *Northumberland*'s mission. She was a lone unit, and possibly no one at the Admiralty really expected very much of her. Lees-Rimington brooded as he sat hunched in his chair on the compass platform. What a pity the country hadn't woken up earlier to its dangers in the thirties, what a pity a huge naval construction programme hadn't been put in hand. They were doing their best now, with cruisers and destroyers and smaller craft being laid down by the minute, but it was almost too late to fill the yawning gaps. If there had been more ships available, some could have been spared to seek out and sink the *Oberhausen*. It was the same with the RAF: not enough planes, not enough pilots and aircrews, and those that were available were never in the right place at the right time. Lees-Rimington switched his useless thoughts and brooded instead on the *Oberhausen* itself.

She could be half an ocean away though he didn't believe she was; and his ship's company would be tiring. Tired men wouldn't fight so well when the time came. Lees-Rimington was certain that time would come, and soon. It was no more than an inner feeling; there was little to back it in hard factual terms. They had not been sighted by any aircraft – nothing had been flying in the vicinity, nothing at all – so the German wouldn't have been receiving any further sighting reports to put him on track. Currently the seas were clear so far as the poor visibility allowed anyone to see. Lees-Rimington let the dawn grow into a dim daylight with the ship still closed up at full action stations, then he spoke.

'Officer of the Watch?'

'Sir?' Cameron was dead tired by now, having difficulty in keeping his eyelids apart after a long night on the bridge.

'Pass the word to the director – the turrets' crews and magazine parties may sleep at their guns or wherever. One man in each position to remain awake. The same with the damage control parties.'

'Aye, aye, sir.'

'And there'll be a relieve-decks for breakfast. Pass that to the Commander – no, wait, Cameron. Ask him to come to the compass platform.'

'Aye, aye, sir.'

Cameron passed the message for the Commander down the voice-pipe to the quartermaster in the wheelhouse, and a boatswain's mate was despatched on his errand. The orders for the partial stand-down were given to the Gunnery Control Officer. In the turrets, in the damage control positions and elsewhere throughout the ship, men dropped to the deck where they stood and mostly fell asleep at once with a sea-man's ability to snatch a bit of kip under all conditions. In the shell-handling room aft the fat three-badge AB had been asleep all night and sod it: he wasn't as young as he'd been once. Contrary-wise, Stripey Barnard chose the moment of sleep to wake up and found himself saddled with the nasty business of being the man to remain awake while the others had their turn. Now he would get a late breakfast and he needed to go to the heads, what was more.

He shouted up the shaft, where the leading hand of the handling-room party was taking it nice and easy. 'Killick!'

A face looked over the lip of the hatch. 'Yep?'

'Want to go to the 'eads.'

There was a laugh. 'We all know you, Stripey. Pee in your pants if the need grows too urgent.'

Stripey swore; the air was blue. 'Some people,' he said witheringly to no one in particular. 'Brought up in a sewer, dirty sod.'

On the compass platform the Commander, starched-cuffed still, obeying the summons, reported briskly to the Captain. He saluted with a snap.

'Good morning, sir!'

'Ah, Commander. Commander, relieve decks for breakfast if you please – see to that at once.'

'Aye, aye, sir.'

'But first, look down there.'

The Commander raised an eyebrow. 'Look where, sir?'

'Where I said – down there. Clearly to be seen in my binoculars.' Lees-Rimington pointed over the guardrail, down towards the jackstaff in the eyes of the ship. The staff had been lowered flat to the deck when the ship had cleared for action, to give an uncluttered field of fire for the guns. 'See what I mean?'

'No, sir.' The Commander peered anxiously, looking efficient.

'The jackstaff – oil on the wood,' Lees-Rimington said. He sounded irritable. 'God knows where it came from. Remove it.'

'In this weather, sir?'

'The weather has nothing to do with it, Commander. I gave an order. Kindly obey it.'

'There's danger to life—'

'Commander, I dislike being argued with on my own bridge.' Lees-Rimington turned his back.

The Commander shrugged and saluted. If he pressed too far, there would be much danger to himself, but he didn't like the order at all. He sent his attendant messenger to the Chief Boatswain's Mate with orders to remove oil pronto from the recumbent jackstaff and within the next few minutes the Chief Boatswain's Mate was talking, none too softly, about bloodly lunatics and murderers. Along with the laying-down of the jackstaff, the fo'c'sle guardrails had been removed and the wind-swept, spray-drenched deck, lurching about, heaving, rising and falling to the scend of the gale-driven sea, was wide open. One slip and you were away. The skipper had to be mad, or maybe it was the Commander off his own bat. The suggestion that it might be the Commander came from the Petty Officer of the Fo'c'sle Division, but the Chief Buffer disagreed.

He said, 'Not on your Aunt Fanny. The Bloke, he never has had an original idea of his own, and this one's as original as sin. No, it come from the skipper, must've, it's just like him.'

'What you going to do about it, Buff?'

'Go meself. I'm not ordering hands out there. Care to volunteer with me?'

'You and you and you?'

'No. No pressure. Up to you.'

'Bugger it,' PO Coomber said. 'Doesn't leave no bloody option, does it?'

Lees-Rimington took his breakfast on the compass platform; his servant brought up eggs and bacon, toast and marmalade, and a steaming pot of coffee with tinned milk. Cameron, as yet awaiting his own relief, felt hunger gnawing. The Captain rejected the eggs and bacon; his stomach was a bath of acid. 'Pig bin,' he said, though it would be a long time before any pigs could benefit from the *Northumberland*'s waste, which in fact would be jettisoned as gash. Drinking coffee, Lees-Rimington looked down at the fo'c'sle. Out into the wind and weather, past the gun-turret immediately before the compass platform, moved two oilskinned and sou'westered figures with knife lanyards tied around their waists to keep their oilskins secured against the gale. They lurched and staggered; one of them lost his footing and slithered towards the unprotected side of the ship as the deck lifted heavily to port. Lees-Rimington stared down; the pain in his stomach worsened. The man saved himself, getting a hand-hold just in time, and clawed and slid his way for'ard as the bows dipped. Suddenly Lees-Rimington heard the cry from the port lookout:

'Ship bearing red eight-five, sir!'

Every eye on the compass platform swung to port; the binoculars went up. A grim, grey shape had emerged from the overcast. The Captain said, 'Identification, Pilot?'

'It's a German heavy cruiser, sir. Bound to be the *Oberhausen*.'

Lees-Rimington nodded, his lips compressed into a bloodless line. Without radar, so little warning in poor visibility! He said, 'Close up all men to their stations immediately, Cameron. Chief Yeoman?'

'Sir?'

'Break out the battle ensigns.' Lees-Rimington leaned over the fore rail of the compass platform and cupped his hands around his mouth. 'You there, those men. Come back instantly. Leave the jackstaff.'

One of the men turned. A hand waved in acknowledgement and they began making their way back to safety. As they did so the Royal Marine bugler put his bugle to the tannoy's microphone and the harsh notes of General Quarters sounded through the cruiser, along the upper deck, in the engine-rooms and boiler-rooms, in the messdecks, in the sick bay. Breakfasts were left uneaten, men poured from the heads and doubled back to their stations. As the great battle ensigns broke from the mastheads, flaunting British sea power towards the German some five miles off the port quarter, the *Northumberland*'s four twin turrets swung in director firing upon the enemy. As the Captain gave the order to the Gunnery Control Officer to open, a rippling line of flame and gunsmoke was seen along the upper deck of the German.

4

TALL and stiff, quite fearless, the Captain stood in the fore part of the compass platform staring through his binoculars at the German. Already he had authorized the breaking of wireless silence, and the signal had gone out in plain language under the Most Immediate prefix: ADMIRALTY REPEATED C-IN-C HOME FLEET FROM NORTHUMBERLAND, I AM UNDER ATTACK BY HEAVY CRUISER OBERHAUSEN IN POSITION 35 DEGREES 30 MINUTES WEST 38 DEGREES NORTH.

It was a matter for conjecture now. Assistance, unless there happened to be a warship at hand in the South Atlantic, couldn't possibly reach them in time, no one was in any doubt about that obvious fact. The signal had been made chiefly to enable Admiral Tovey's Home Fleet to converge later upon the *Oberhausen*, to intercept and sink her before she had beaten it back to Brest. In the meantime, the *Northumberland* was fighting for her life, sending her shells flinging across the tumultuous seas whenever the guns could be brought to bear on their target. In fact, for a good deal of the time those guns were staring straight down into the water as the cruiser rolled violently, and so far no hits had been observed on the German, storming through the water under the Nazi swastika emblazoned upon her naval ensign. Lees-Rimington was twisting his command this way and that in order to avoid the Nazi gunfire. It was intense and would have been deadly accurate had it not been for the sea that was running: the bad weather was against them as much as it was against the *Northumberland*.

Below decks the din of battle thudded and echoed, making the plates ring like an orchestra from Mars. In the starboard for'ard engine-room, one of four mighty palaces of power which drove the shafts, turned the screws and sent the cruiser flinging through the water to keep her distance from the enemy, the Commander(E) stood on the starting-platform, clad in white overalls and holding a pad of cotton-waste clenched in a fist. His face was impassive as he looked down on the shining brass of gauges and handwheels, on white-painted, lagged steam pipes, on the ERAs and stokers moving about their work as though nothing was happening above, the ERAs watching the dials and feeling bearings, the stokers using their oil-cans here and there. Down here, there was nothing they could do but keep the screws turning and hope that the ship wouldn't lift against an oncoming Hun shell that might penetrate the port-side engine-rooms and turn them into an earthbound hell.

Likewise in the boiler-rooms. In one of these, the Stoker Petty Officer in charge of his particular black gang, though not so black as they'd been when they shovelled coal into the furnaces, wiped a rag across his streaming face and thought back to Jutland, where he'd been a Stoker Second Class in one of Beatty's old battle-cruisers, a coal burner as it had happened. They'd shovelled coal then, all right! Their lives had depended upon keeping steam on the main engines. Clad in filthy singlets and once-white duck trousers, with sweat-bands round their foreheads, they had been urged on to superhuman efforts by a Chief Stoker whose command of foul language was admired throughout the whole of the Grand Fleet. A shell from a German High Seas Fleet battleship had entered that boiler-room, and Stoker Second Class Lockett, now Stoker PO Lockett, hauled back to active service from pension and the Royal Fleet Reserve, wondered even now how he had managed to live. He'd been the only one in the boiler-room who had and he couldn't remember a lot about it. There had been searing flame and the bloody furnace had split open; there had been scalding steam when the pipes fractured and then, or so he had been told after, the North Sea had come in and done the ship a bit of temporary good, and no doubt him too. Funny things happened when shells struck, as with bombs. You simply never knew. Lockett believed he could have been shielded from the worst by a twisted bulk-head and then sort of floated out through the hole, to be picked up' by one of the cutters after the battle-cruiser went down.

All he knew was that he'd been through hell fire and had survived. He could hardly expect to be lucky twice, and that knowledge was responsible for about fifty per cent of the sweat pouring from his body. He prayed. God, who didn't live in a place like this, might have mercy on him after all. Twice would be a bit much, though, come to think of it, God might relent: he hadn't had much of a life, not really – pension so small you couldn't see it, no jobs going in the thirties, and a missus like the Rock of Gibraltar.

That was when the ship's side lifted, and the shell hit.

'Hit aft, sir.' The voice came up the voice-pipe; Cameron reported to the Captain.

'Damage?'

The further reports were coming up; Cameron passed them on. 'Shell entered Number Two boiler-room, sir, but failed to explode. Damage control parties are plugging the hole now, sir.'

'Casualties?'

'The Stoker PO, sir.'

Lees-Rimington nodded. 'Starboard twenty.' They had to keep twisting.

'Starboard twenty, sir.' Cameron passed the order down and the *Northumberland* swung heavily, presenting her stern to the enemy. In this position only her after turrets could bear; Lees-Rimington, staring aft, brought her round again. The guns crashed out in a salvo, banging throughout the ship.

In the wheelhouse below, the Chief Quartermaster

said through set teeth, 'Mad sod. Wants to commit suicide. We're bloody outgunned and we'd do a bloody sight better to run.'

'Cameron,' Lees-Rimington said crisply; he happened to be standing close to the voice-pipe. The Chief QM's speech had been loud.

'Yes, sir?'

'Did you hear that?'

'Er—'

'I heard it, therefore you did. Pass down to the Chief Quartermaster, he's relieved from the wheel. The leading hand will take over. As soon as we break off action, the Chief Quartermaster is to be brought before the Officer of the Watch and placed in the Commander's report.'

'I don't think it was meant to be overheard, sir—'

'Grow up, Cameron. And don't argue with your Captain.' Lees-Rimington turned forward again, his hands clenched into fists, his stomach causing him intense pain and a raw, sick feeling rising all the way up his chest. He would not tolerate defeatism in a senior chief petty officer. The British Fleet did not run. He would continue the action to the death. A few minutes later more detailed reports reached the compass platform. In Number Two boiler-room all was now well. The hole had been successfully plugged and the space was being pumped out. The furnaces were burning still; water had entered only when the ship rolled to port. Stoker PO Lockett, who had taken the full weight of the unexploded eight-inch shell, had been flattened against a watertight bulkhead. There was nothing left of him except strawberry jam from the chest upwards. There were no other casualties. Once again Lees-Rimington nodded. This time he said, 'Poor devil. He was blown up at Jutland. It's bad luck.'

Cameron felt surprise: he hadn't expected the Captain to be *au fait* with any of his ship's company's past. It didn't seem quite like him. Half a minute later, the *Oberhausen* scored another hit. The *Northumberland*'s after funnel vanished in a shower of fragmented metal and fire broke out on the after superstructure. This time, there were many casualties.

The dead had been left to lie where they were or to roll shapelessly into the sea, which was where they would have gone in due course anyway. Those yet living had to come first. They were attended on the spot by the Surgeon Lieutenant. Dr Field had qualified at Bart's only the year before. He'd never seen anything like this and he had a job not to be sick as he did what he could for torn-off limbs and swabbed at virtually gutted stomachs that had been sliced by the cruel jags of shell fragments or funnel-metal. There was smoke and fire and steam all round him too, helping to confuse the issue. Some of the seamen were screaming, pleading: most of them were around twenty years of age.

The Sick Berth CPO, Haventon, was a tower of strength and very phlegmatic. He took charge, advising the doctor until he moved incautiously, tripped, and went headlong down the hole where the funnel had been. Haventon's screams, like those of the youngsters, ripped up from an invisible hell until the fire and the smoke kippered his carcase as he hung from some jagged steel. Dr Field was aghast, none of his medical knowledge any use to CPO Haventon. He shook like a leaf. Covered with blood, not his own, he swung round and waved both balled fists towards the bridge.

'Murderer!' he screamed into the gale. *'Bloody murderer!'*

The wind direction was kind to him as the *Northumberland* executed another turn: this time, the Captain didn't hear. The shout had relieved the doctor's feelings a little and he took a grip, did what he could. After first aid, totally inadequate really, the wounded were removed to the sick bay and came under the care of the PMO. He had never seen anything like it either. Road casualties hadn't been quite so gruesome in his experience; usually, they hadn't been burned as well and there were never so many of them all at once.

Ordinary Seaman Jones stared from his cot and was sick on the deck. He'd wanted to get up when the action started but neither his back nor the PMO would let him. There was a dreadful, appalling stench of blood and ether. He'd never seen death before; and now it all came to him vividly, much more vividly than at the time, how his father and his two brothers must have died, in agony like this. He stared like a ghost; the sick bay shook and rattled around him as the screws thundered and the guns crashed out. Fragments of cork insulation flew like confetti, and from a rack a couple of bottles fell and broke on the deck. Through the door, helping to carry the wounded, came the padre in his dog-collar, looking ashen: John Harvey was RNVR and had come from a country rectory in Cambridgeshire. The war was shaking everyone up cruelly. On the other hand, this was real; God's work was being done with a vengeance now. Succour was the watchword.

There were more hits: a number of the boats had gone, and there was fire in the Captain's quarters aft. The Royal Marine sentry had been killed as he stood guard over the rifle-racks. The fire parties hadn't yet subdued the fire and it was spreading for'ard along the cabin flat towards the hatch over the magazine and shell-handling room aft. All this, the Commander reported by sound-powered telephone to the compass platform. The Captain spoke to him.

The Commander said, 'I think we should turn our tails to them, sir, present a smaller target.'

'No, Commander. The opposite! I intend to turn towards.'

'I see, sir. Towards . . . you mean to *ram*?' The voice carried incredulity.

'Precisely, Commander, yes. Now – the after magazine and handling room. Just how bad is it?'

'On a knife-edge, sir. I'd advise evacuating all personnel from the after—'

'Nonsense, Commander, my after turrets are still in action and I need the men below. You must stand by to flood if and when necessary.' Lees-Rimington put the receiver back on its hook and turned to Cameron. 'Port twenty,' he said.

'Port twenty, sir.'

The order was repeated from the wheelhouse and the *Northumberland* began to swing towards the German cruiser. Lees-Rimington stared ahead again, hands clasped behind his back. Then he moved to the tannoy to broadcast a warning to the ship's company. He said, 'This is your Captain speaking. Stand by to ram.' He switched off and called the director. 'Gunnery Control Officer ... all guns that can bear will continue firing until the last second. Until the end.' He hung up and went back to his forward-looking position. Hurtling on and spitting flame from the fore turrets, the *Northumberland* closed the gap towards the final crump that would shatter her. Lees-Rimington looked up at the streaming battle ensigns ... the British Fleet never retreated, it kept the seas. As a concept that was overridingly important – both to impress the enemy and to hearten the rest of the Fleet with the knowledge that they were pre-eminent upon the seas and made not as lesser men were made. Yes, it was very important for morale, as Captain Kennedy of the *Rawalpindi* had known, as had Captain Fogarty Fegen of the *Jervis Bay*. True, they had had a patrol to cover, a convoy to guard, as he had not. For a fleeting moment Lees-Rimington felt a nagging doubt: he had not the justification of Kennedy or Fogarty Fegen for sending his ship's company to their certain death. But he cast the doubt aside. The only alternatives were to be a simple target for the German gunners, or to surrender. And he would never strike his flag. It was all inevitable.

Strangely, the German fire had been suspended.

Lees-Rimington was puzzled by that. Perhaps they had been taken by surprise ... the telephone shrilled its high whine from the cabin flat aft. It was the Commander again.

'Yes? Captain here.'

'Fire's right over the handling-room hatch, sir.'

'Flood, Commander. Flood at once.'

'The men, sir—'

'I know about the men, Commander.'

Lees-Rimington put down the telephone. When fire spread, you had to think about the ship, and there was no time to unclip the hatch and bring the men up. If you unclipped and opened the hatch, fire could blow the ship to fragments. Lees-Rimington brought up his glasses and stared ahead as his ship raced for the enemy. There was something odd going on: the *Northumberland*'s fore turrets were still firing; they had scored a number of hits when Lees-Rimington had first put his ship on her ramming course, but now the German was turning away, narrowing the target, whilst not returning the British fire. Then something else was seen, reported from the gunnery control position: aircraft with British naval markings, some half-dozen of them, emerging from the cloud cover. As they were seen, the *Oberhausen* went into action with all her ack-ack armament, blazing away into the sky. But the planes of the Fleet Air Arm made their bombing runs, flying crazily through the bursting shrapnel, and the German was taken from stem to stern by a stick of bombs. As her decks erupted in flame and smoke, there was a shout from one of the *Northumberland*'s bridge lookouts:

'Torpedo-bombers attacking now, sir!'

Cameron and the Captain watched in awe. Four old Swordfish biplanes were seen to be coming in low over the heavy seas, heading for the German's port side. By this time, thanks to the impact of the bombs, the *Oberhausen* was virtually at the mercy of the old Stringbags, with few guns still in action. The aircraft came in steadily, released their torpedoes, and then lifted over the German's decks. As they came on above the *Northumberland*, Lees-Rimington took off his cap and waved it vigorously. From the leader, a hand was raised in acknowledgement. A moment later, three more explosions rocked the German and stopped her in her tracks.

Lees-Rimington said, 'Belay ramming. Telegraphs to slow ahead, starboard twenty.'

The sight had been an appalling one: the *Oberhausen*, hit by the torpedoes in her vital parts, went sky high as her magazines exploded. Debris was rocketed into the air, to fall back like hail on the sea and on the *Northumberland*'s decks.

What was left of her settled and sank inside sixty seconds, leaving a confused vortex of water which the rearing waves quickly covered. There were few survivors: just some thirty or forty men who had been thrown clear from the upper deck. Lees-Rimington moved in with scrambling-nets over the sides and picked up as many as could haul themselves aboard: with a British aircraft-carrier and its planes in the vicinity no U-boats would be surfacing even if their commanders had seen any point in doing so: rough seas were not conducive to U-boat activity. The German seamen were brought aboard half dead, with no fight left in them at all. Many had been badly burned, and were attended to by the medical staff. They were Nazis but professionalism took over. In the sick bay the padre looked at them wonderingly and thanked God for many blessings received that day. It had been, in his view, God's work that had saved the *Northumberland*.

On his emergence from the after shell-handling room into the cabin flat, Stripey Barnard looked in awe at the burned paintwork. There was still a strong stench of burning but the fires were out: the fire parties had got the situation under control just in time – just in time for the Commander to take it upon himself to belay the order to flood the after magazine. Stripey Barnard didn't realize how close he and his mates had come to drowning until he was made aware of it by a petty officer, and then he lived through the scene he hadn't had to take part in: he saw his body being forced up by the mounting water as the valves were opened, gasping for the last tiny fragment of air as his face met the cold unyielding steel of the clipped-down hatch, the hatch that couldn't be opened from underneath. One man, just one man, had given the flooding order on a whim: Lees-Rimington, who would have killed him and the others had the order gone ahead. Stripey Barnard took a deep breath but held on to his opinion of the skipper when he saw the PO's eye on him.

On the compass platform Lees-Rimington took the reports from his heads of departments: there had been the damage along the upper deck, whilst below most of the officers' cabins had been either gutted by fire or drenched with water or both. Some of the wireless aerials had gone but the CPO Telegraphist could cope with that without too much difficulty. Apart from the small hole and Stoker PO Lockett, all was well in the engine-rooms and boiler-rooms. The ship was seaworthy.

The Commander, eyebrows singed and uniform filthy, spoke of the casualties. 'Twenty-three dead, forty-two wounded, sir. Nearly all of them upper deck personnel.'

'Gunnery rates, Commander?'

'Largely, sir, yes. We'll need replacements ... also we've expended a lot of ammunition.'

'So my Gunnery Officer tells me. So your suggestion is?'

The Commander appeared surprised at being asked. He said, 'Return to base, sir. We're not that far out yet, and repairs—'

'Return to the Clyde, Commander?'

'I'd say so, sir.'

'Nonsense! I shall do no such thing. I have my orders and my ship is seaworthy, still well capable of being fought.'

'The cabins, sir—'

'Unimportant – my officers can rough it without coming to harm, Commander. We shall make for Freetown in Sierra Leone for replenishments. Pilot?'

'Sir?'

'Lay off a course for Freetown,' Lees-Rimington said briskly, rubbing his hands together. 'Commander, make your arrangements for committal of the dead – I shall conduct a service as soon as the sailmaker has finished with the hammocks. In the meantime, you may relax the ship's company. You may go to cruising stations. Cameron?'

'Yes, sir?'

'Send down for the Master-at-Arms. He's to bring the Chief Quartermaster before you as Officer of the Watch.'

5

THERE was a curious feeling throughout the ship now, not a happy one: their chestnuts had been pulled from the fire by the Fleet Air Arm, not by the Captain, who would have killed them all by ramming. The skipper had been dead lucky to have been forestalled. The older men, the RN and Fleet Reserve ratings, were fairly phlegmatic about it, being steeped in the ways of captains and their notions of keeping the Fleet in being and all that. It was the hostilities-only men who were bitter about it and who didn't see it in the same light at all. They doubted if the impact of the *Northumberland* would have done more than dent the German's armoured belt in any case, unless she had taken the *Oberhausen* right for'ard, which the German would surely have been astute enough to avoid.

Some of them witnessed the unusual sight of a Chief Petty Officer being marched to the compass platform by the Master-at-Arms – there was little doubt that he was being marched, not just accompanied: you could always tell when the MAA, officious sod, was shepherding a miscreant. It was something in his unctuous expression, his gait, the very way in which he held his clipboard out in front of him – unmistakable. Of course, the buzz had already spread and the lower deck mostly agreed with the Chief QM: the skipper *was* bloody mad and it was unfair to shove the Chief QM in the rattle for telling the truth.

As he waited on the compass platform for the formalities of the charge to be gone through, Cameron felt much the same but knew there was nothing he could do about it. He was simply the initial vehicle by which the Chief QM would be punished ultimately. His hope was that the Captain would relent somewhere along the way, along the routine as laid down for defaulters by King's Regulations and Admiralty Instructions. He might tell the Commander to dismiss the case, or utter a caution, when it came before him – though Cameron doubted this. When a case was initiated by the Captain, any captain, it wasn't usually disposed of *en route* ...

'Officer o' the Watch, sir?'

The MAA, puffing from his exertions up the ladders, had reached the bridge. 'Yes, Master?'

'Defaulter, sir.' The MAA said this loudly so that it reached the Captain. The Captain should not overhear the preliminaries of a case that he would ultimately have to judge himself.

Lees-Rimington turned from the fore guardrail. MAA Pond saluted, and the Captain returned the gesture formally, his face hard. 'I shall be in my sea-cabin, Mr Cameron,' he said. 'Call me in accordance with standing orders if and when necessary.'

'Aye, aye, sir.'

Lees-Rimington stalked away; the lookouts looked out ostentatiously, ears flapping nevertheless. It wasn't every day a senior rating was put in the report. The Yeoman of the Watch found something needing attention on the flag deck, and slid down the ladder on the palms of his hands, feet clear of the treads. MAA Pond cleared his throat and jerked his head at Cameron, indicating the starboard wing. Cameron took the hint and accompanied the MAA out of earshot of the defaulter. MAA Pond rumbled into his ear. 'The charge, sir. The wording, see. I've 'ad words with the Chief QM. We 'ave to get it right, like, sir.'

Cameron side-stepped it, wisely. 'What do you advise, Master?'

'Yessir.' Pond had known the officer would say that. The

52

RNVR, they hadn't the experience, but they did know they could easily balls-up a charge by a word out of place and then the wrath of Almighty God wearing four straight stripes would fall upon them. Pond went on, 'Did utter insubordinate and disloyal words such that if over'eard by the enemy could give succour to the latter. We then adds the words, sir. All right, sir?'

'That's in accordance with the Captain's wishes, is it?'

'Yessir. If you would repeat the words you over'eard, sir, I'll write 'em down like.'

Cameron repeated the words. 'Let's get it over, Master.'

'Yessir.' MAA Pond marched away and arranged the Chief QM in the port wing. Then he marched back and saluted Cameron. 'Officer o' the Watch, sir. Defaulter, sir. Chief Petty Officer Thomas, sir. Will-you-'ear-the-case-if-you-please-sir.'

'Very well,' Cameron said.

Pond saluted again and turned about. He marched away, then came back with the Chief QM. The rigmarole went on its way. 'Off cap.' The Chief QM removed his cap. 'Herbert Arthur Thomas, sir, Chief Petty Officer Royal Fleet Reserve, Official Number P/JX 187153. Did at ...' He consulted the notes on his clipboard. 'Did at 0838 hours this morning utter insubordinate and disloyal words such that if over'eard by the enemy could give succour to the latter, namely, mad sod, wants to commit suicide, we're bloody outgunned and we'd do a bloody sight better to run, sir. The reference being to the Captain, sir.'

'I see,' Cameron said, repressing a strong desire to laugh at the MAA's tone. He addressed the Chief QM. 'Have you anything you wish to say, Chief?'

Chief Petty Officer Thomas, rigidly at attention, stared straight ahead over Cameron's shoulder. 'No, sir.'

'I should warn you I overheard the words myself and will be called as a witness.'

'Yes, sir.'

'You still wish to say nothing?'

'That's right, sir. I reserves me defence, sir.'

Cameron nodded. 'Commander's report,' he said, this being all he could say.

MAA Pond said, 'Remanded to Commander's report. On cap, salute the officer, about turn, double march, down the ladder. Thank you, sir.' Once again he saluted, then followed the culprit down to the upper deck. Cameron tried to forget the matter; in his mouth it tasted sour. Thomas was a man with much to lose and his pension could be affected if the Captain so willed it in his eventual punishment. In the meantime, Thomas would sail the seas with it all hanging over him; the Captain was unlikely to hold defaulters until the ship reached Freetown, and the Commander had yet to be gone through first. The trial-and-judgment routine of the Navy dragged its feet....

Lees-Rimington came back to the compass platform, making no reference to what had gone on in his absence. The cruiser steamed on, throwing back the still heavy seas from her forefoot as she shouldered the waves.

The weather moderated as the *Northumberland* came into the tropics. The ship's company shifted into their white uniforms: white cap covers, white shirts and shorts – tropical rig, known in the Navy as number thirteens. Now they sweltered; there seemed to be no air at all, just blazing sun and blue, unruffled sea, a striking contrast to the earlier part of the run. The ship was murder below, an overheated tin kettle, for the sea itself warmed her from beneath. The messdecks began to smell of feet and body sweat. At night the watch below lay soaking wet in their hammocks, and the officers, now mainly in hammocks themselves following the fire's wreckage in the cabins, took cold baths at hourly intervals to relieve the onset of prickly heat. There were not enough baths on the lower deck to allow the ratings such a luxury, and they suffered badly. The Commander, making his night rounds behind the MAA and a bugler, held a handkerchief to his nose all the way through the messdecks, bending his head beneath the slung hammocks and wondering how in God's name the poor beggars put up with it. It was almost the smell of death.

Dropping south, they raised Cape Sierra Leone at the entry to the Rokel River, and steamed slowly and carefully in between the twisting sandbanks under the direction of the Navigating Officer. Lees-Rimington was exercising his right as an officer of the Royal Navy not to take a pilot: he would not trust the natives, and he had rejected the signalled offer of pilotage from the depôt ship on station off Government Wharf. As the cruiser nosed in and the palm-covered hillsides of the shore began to close them in, Stripey Barnard, who had been to Freetown before, identified the floating barrack-stanchions. 'Depôt ship's the *Edinburgh Castle*,' he said to his winger. 'Ex Union Castle liner. The other's the store ship ... *Philoctetes*. We used to call 'er the Feel-her-Titties. Both the buggers fast aground on their own gash. Don't go to sea no more, they don't.'

From the flag deck the signals were already being made: Lees-Rimington, who intended to proceed to sea again as soon as possible, was stating his requirements: seamen replacements, gunnery rates if possible; ammunition for his eight-inch guns; and oil fuel. The Paymaster wanted fresh fruit and nuts and could do with some Carnation tinned milk. As the *Northumberland* let go her anchor and was brought up, dug-out canoes came from the shore in swarms. The Kroos of Sierra Leone were a fishing race, and astute and greedy traders. Many of the canoes were piled high with great bunches of bananas upon which the almost naked Kroos were perched, waving and calling out. Over the side of one canoe a black body dangled, relieving itself.

Lees-Rimington said, 'Filthy place and filthy people.' He leaned over the fore bridge screen. 'Chief Boatswain's Mate!'

The buffer looked up. 'Sir?'

'Hoses. I don't want those people alongside me, much less to try to come aboard. Keep them off.'

'Aye, aye, sir.'

Within two minutes the wash-deck hoses were in action; the wielders of them enjoyed themselves. The Kroos didn't appear to mind very much, and laughed and cat-called in some unintelligible language as the water swished into them, sending one or two tumbling into the muddy river-waters. They didn't come alongside; the white sailors would be given shore leave in due course and could be robbed then. But the Kroos were to be cheated of their prey. A hand-message was brought from the base for the Captain, a sealed envelope marked By Hand of Officer and carried by a lieutenant RN who climbed aboard from a skimmer and was taken to the cuddy.

Orders? Speculation ran through the ship. The bearer of the message departed and then the tannoy came on and the boatswain's mate's voice sounded ominous: 'Do you hear there ... shore leave will not be piped. The ship is under sailing orders. Shore leave will not be piped. The ship is under sailing orders.'

The tannoy clicked off.

Ten minutes later the Captain's galley was called away, and was brought smartly from the lower boom to the starboard quarterdeck ladder. Lees-Rimington embarked with his Navigating Officer and proceeded inshore to Government Wharf under a blazing sun, dressed in beautifully starched number tens with the tunic's high white collar setting off the formidable line of his jaw. There were puckers of pain around his eyes and the mouth was pulled into a thin, bloodless line: his stomach nagged, had scarcely ceased nagging since before the *Northumberland* had left the Clyde. That kind of pain was not good for a Captain with high responsibilities and a constant need for unimpaired judgment; Lees-Rimington, looking back at his camouflage-painted ship, remembered that he had yet to hold Captain's Defaulters and that the Chief Quartermaster had been referred from Commander's Defaulters the previous day. Possibly his initiation of that charge had been an error of judgment, but to admit that now would be to loosen discipline to some extent and to show his ship's company that he was capable of vascillation. That would never do.

The Captain returned aboard and sent for his heads of departments, giving no clue to the anxious gangway staff as to what had been discussed ashore. Within half an hour of his return, a draft of ratings joined from the depôt ship, Lieutenant Price was removed to mend his broken leg aboard the *Edinburgh Castle* together with all wounded men, the German prisoners were landed, and the Paymaster's fruit and other stores came alongside for'ard to be hoisted inboard. No ammunition: there was no current availability in Freetown and the *Northumberland* would have to proceed to sea without replenishment; she would be able to embark ammunition at the Cape. But before then, Lees-Rimington told his senior officers, the ship was likely to be in action. He had been given news of a raider at large.

'The *Helmut Genscher*,' he said. 'A converted German merchantman. Six 5.9-inch main armament. Plenty of anti-aircraft guns. She has torpedo-tubes as well – four 21-inch – and she carries spotting aircraft, two Heinkel 114s. She's already taken or sunk twenty-two ships. She's known to be somewhere in the South Atlantic. I am under specific orders to bring her to action and sink her.' Lees-Rimington looked at his watch. 'As soon as we've taken oil fuel, we proceed to sea. I shall not hold Defaulters, Commander.'

'The Chief QM, sir—'

'Yes. I repeat, I shall not hold Defaulters. One more thing: C-in-C reports three of our ships in the South Atlantic, proceeding independently for Scottish ports – fast ships. One from Cape Town, one from Montevideo, one from Sydney round Cape Horn. In view of this information, I intend shaping my course south towards Tristan da Cunha. That is all, gentlemen, thank you.'

When the stores lighter left the cruiser's side, an Admiralty oiler came out and secured; the pipelines were connected and the bunkers were topped up to full capacity. Immediately the oiler had cast off and moved away, the cable and side party and special sea dutymen were piped to their stations and the anchor was weighed. *Northumberland* moved out again to sea, her wounds untended, the gaping hole where the after funnel had been shot away covered with a heavy tarpaulin and nothing else, her after flat still gutted and the cabins themselves untenable. Her decks were scarred with shell splinters, the shell-hole in her Number Two boiler-room still carried its makeshift repair. In the interest of getting quickly back to sea all these things had had to be left, and in any case Freetown had few repair facilities.

Soon after the *Northumberland* had rounded Cape Sierra Leone on her southerly course, Lees-Rimington spoke to his ship's company. He told them the facts and added that, by steaming on a mean course southwards, he would be as well placed as he could be to move towards the German raider the moment she was sighted by a possible target and that target broke wireless silence to request assistance.

'We may not get there in time,' he said. 'We may still be too far off. But we shall know where to find the *Helmut Genscher* afterwards. We have already come out well from the attack by the *Oberhausen*. We should find an auxiliary cruiser an easier enemy.'

'You 'ope,' Stripey Barnard said bitterly as the tannoy was switched off. He was still feeling sore about his near death in the shell-handling room, knowing full well that the Captain would do it to him again the moment it suited him. They'd been lucky in the case of the *Oberhausen*; you couldn't expect to be lucky twice. They'd go up in a bloody great sheet of flame and if Stripey Barnard had been the skipper he'd turn north for home and bugger it. But he kept his mouth shut on that point as he saw the Buffer coming along the deck: the Chief QM was already in the rattle for saying something similar and if the skipper could come down on *him* like a load of crap from on high, a poor bloody AB would probably be shot.

.   .   .   .   .

58

At her maximum speed the *Northumberland* dropped south, down into the area where the three independently-routed merchant ships were steaming for home. One was a refrigerated meat ship with a valuable cargo from the Argentine side of the River Plate; the vessel coming up from the Cape was a tanker that had brought aviation spirit from the Persian Gulf to South Africa and was still partly loaded for the Clyde; the third was bringing wheat from Australia round Cape Horn. All three ships were needed urgently in home waters and not only for their cargoes: Britain's losses had been only just short of catastrophic and by this stage of the war every bottom was counting, every sinking was a major loss. The oppressive heat grew worse as the *Northumberland* plunged deeper into the tropics; then, as they came down along the Mid-Atlantic Ridge as shown on the chart and left the South-Eastern Atlantic Basin to port in the latitude of Swakopmund in South-West Africa, the sun left them. They were back in restless waters, with a lowering sky and breaking seas that were cut off in spindrift blowing along a rising south-easterly to bring discomfort to the watchkeepers and turrets' crews as the sweaty, close damp penetrated everywhere. Watch succeeded watch, day and night; a careful lookout was maintained. At one stage, during a dirty night, they passed a north-bound convoy from the Cape, a conglomeration of shipping shepherded by two cruisers and six destroyers, lumbering through the darkness at seven knots. Cameron, who was on watch, called Lees-Rimington in accordance with standing orders; the Captain altered to the westward to avoid running through the centre of the convoy.

It was still dark, although not far off dawn, when the central receiving room buzzed the compass platform.

'Officer of the Watch, sir. Message received from ss *Fountains Abbey*. Reads, "Am in sight of vessel believed to be German raider Helmut Genscher".'

6

ONCE again the sound-powered telephone whined in Lees-Rimington's sea-cabin. Answering immediately and taking Cameron's report, he said, 'For a start, dawn action stations. But use the alarm rattlers, not the bugle.'

'Aye, aye, sir.' Cameron pressed the alarm button. The rattlers sounded throughout the ship indicating that, this dawn, it wasn't mere routine. The urgent noise brought men crashing from their hammocks. Within fifteen seconds of being called, Lees-Rimington was on the compass platform. He stared at Cameron and asked, 'What's the given position of the *Fountains Abbey*? That's the tanker, isn't it?'

'Yes, sir. Latitude 27 degrees 30 minutes south, longitude 15 degrees west, sir.'

'Where's the Navigating Officer? Oh, there you are, Pilot.' Lees-Rimington brought up his binoculars and examined the still-dark horizons ahead and on either bow. 'That position. Put it on the chart.'

The Navigator thrust his head beneath the flap of the chart table and busied himself with a pencil and parallel ruler. He backed out and said, 'Fifteen miles dead ahead, sir.'

Lees-Rimington nodded. 'In that case we maintain our course and speed. Cameron?'

'Sir?'

'Call the engine-room. Tell the Commander(E) that his Captain wishes him to produce every revolution the engines are capable of.'

'Aye, aye, sir.' Cameron passed the message down direct to

60

the starting platform, using the sound-powered telephone. Lees-Rimington remained staring ahead, frowning into the approaching dawn. He was inclined to doubt the accuracy of the report from the *Fountains Abbey*: it was not easy to identify a ship's silhouette in darkness – it was very difficult, in fact. That ship could be almost anything: a neutral, even a British vessel straggled from the convoy they'd passed, or the wheat ship from Australia perhaps, now well around the Horn – only she would have turned north somewhat sooner, probably, rather than head across towards the African coast.

'I'm not convinced,' Lees-Rimington said. 'Warn the director. I shall not open fire on sighting. Not until I'm much more certain.'

As Cameron called up the Gunnery Control Officer in the director, the Navigator put a point of view. He said, 'I think we can take it she's the German, sir—'

'Why?'

'She'll have intercepted the *Fountains Abbey*'s transmission, sir. If she's not the raider, she'd have said so. Then the *Fountains Abbey* would have sent out a negative.',

'Not unless her master's a fool,' Lees-Rimington snapped. 'I wouldn't expect him to place any credence whatsoever in such a signal ... although I agree with you, the ship might well make it. True or false would not emerge until too late.' He steadied his binoculars again, concentrating ahead as the cruiser rushed onwards, faster now, flinging back the sea in a bow wave that hissed in spume down either side of the hull. He stepped to the tannoy. 'This is your Captain speaking. The ship may be in action within the next half-hour. We may have the *Helmut Genscher* in our sights, but I don't promise it.'

'*Promise* it,' Stripey Barnard said witheringly, down in the after shell-handling room. 'What's 'e think 'e is, Father Christmas?'

Once again the sick bay was empty of all cot cases except for Ordinary Seaman Jones, had been so ever since the wounded men had been transferred at Freetown. All Jones needed was bed rest, no point in landing him. Price had been a different kettle of fish: the leg wasn't mending well at all. The PMO, having made his rounds of the emergency dressing stations, was back in the sick bay when the Chaplain entered. 'He brought solidity with him: he was built like a bull. 'Here if needed, PMO,' he said.

'Let's hope you won't be. I don't fancy this much . . . after last time!'

The padre grinned. 'There's a certain inevitability, you must admit.'

'About death, d'you mean?'

'Well, that too, of course. But I didn't mean quite that. In the words of a rather stupid song, we're here because we're here because we're here. Because we have to be.'

'Oh God, I know all that . . . sorry!'

The padre waved a hand. 'Please don't apologize, PMO. This isn't a bad moment to call upon God, as a matter of fact. You and I, and your staff, are the ones who're going to be doing his work if we go into action.' He smiled, looking almost boyish. 'I may have said the same thing before – I'm getting repetitive in my old age.'

'But you mean it, don't you?'

'Yes, I mean it. Very much so. In a sense we can hope to redress the balance. There's so much evil in the world, in the war. What you do – not so much me, in fact I'm pretty useless in the view of most of the ship's company, but you – it shines like a light.' The padre stopped there; he had no option. There had been a violent concussion right alongside and a little below the sick bay and everything seemed to be heaving about.

The PMO said, 'Oh, Jesus Christ,' and this time didn't apologize. He found himself flat on the deck with everything broken around him. There was a smell of ether, and of burning, the deck was listing and water was lapping up through the split corticene. Blood was everywhere. The padre, a bucolic man with a big red face, was as white as a sheet. Drained of

62

blood – literally. The PMO's medical mind ticked over: one of the padre's carotid arteries had gone, succumbing, no doubt, to a sliver of splintered metal.

As the deck swayed, the PMO got to his feet and groped for some support. There were voices, loudly raised. The burning smell increased and, from the slopping water, steam rose into the air. There was screaming – he'd only just realized it was coming from inside the sick bay. It was young Jones. The PMO lurched across to his cot: there wasn't much left of it, and what there was had been forced through Jones' body. He hadn't got long to live, probably only minutes, though they would seem like hours. On the other side of the cot, the LSBA lay with his back twisted like a corkscrew and his head, or rather his neck, nipped in a section of steel deck that had risen in a hump, and split. He was dead. And Jones . . . the PMO breathed hard and felt the onset of sheer panic. Then he pulled himself together and dealt with Jones' agony the only way he could: with shaking fingers he took up a syringe, plunged it into a phial of morphine, drew the liquid up, went over to the cot, and gave the injection. He wondered whether or not the padre would have approved of that, whether or not that particular deed would shine before God. Whether it did or whether it didn't, he believed himself to have done right.

Having done it, he left the sick bay. He was too shaken to realize what he was doing, where he was going: when he left the compartment via what had been the doorway, he felt his feet fall away from him and he dropped like a stone into searing fire.

Lees-Rimington stared from the compass platform. He was calling himself all kinds of a fool: he'd been too damned certain in his own mind that considerable doubt must exist. As a result, he'd delayed too long in giving the order for his guns to open. The suspect ship hadn't looked like the silhouettes he had seen of the *Helmut Genscher*. In fact, she had looked totally different – until her fake superstructure and other off-putting devices had been very suddenly swept aside to reveal menacing gun-barrels, and the battle ensigns of the Third Reich had been run up to the mastheads. She had gone into action with the most extraordinary swiftness and efficiency – gone into action, moreover, against both her adversaries. The *Fountains Abbey* had blown up immediately as a result of a hit smack in one of her aviation spirit tanks, gone up in a ball of spreading flame and thick, black smoke, and had sunk almost at once. Prior to this, a torpedo from the German had taken the *Northumberland* and smashed a large hole in her starboard side and she was now listing badly. She was able to fire her guns, though. And she was giving back as good as she was taking. Shell for shell ... and her guns were the heavier, besides which she carried eight against six.

A ramrod against the fore screen of the compass platform, Lees-Rimington watched his shells take the German raider. A mast went, crashing in flames over the side. A dull glow spread from where the mast had driven down through the deck: there was fire aboard the *Helmut Genscher*. Lees-Rimington was taking a risk now: he had swung the *Northumberland* broadside to the enemy so that all his eight-inch turrets could bear, and she was taking heavy punishment as a result, but the movement of the ship beneath him – sluggish, inert – had told him she wasn't going to last long in any case. The torpedo had done immense damage below. But Lees-Rimington was going to go down fighting. His guns crashed out: then X turret aft took a direct hit right between the twin eight-inch barrels. The steel plates glowed red: Lees-Rimington watched in horror. The guns' crews must have fried. The turret blew up in an inferno of smoke and flame. Then, behind the Captain, Cameron made a report.

'Torpedo trail, sir, coming towards the port bow!'

Lees-Rimington looked. He saw the submerged menace carving its path towards the ship, saw the line of disturbed water clearly. His ship was handling too sluggishly now for him to turn her away in time; and he meant to keep his guns bearing in any case. He said, 'All engines, emergency full astern.'

'All engines, emergency full astern, sir!' Cameron passed the order down.

Bells rang below in the wheelhouse as the four brass handles were pulled over. In the engine-rooms the great spinning shafts were stopped and reversed as quickly as possible. A shudder ran through the ship, juddering her plates as the way began to come off. Too slowly ... on the compass platform Lees-Rimington staggered back as the second torpedo took the bow. Cameron caught him in his arms as the huge concussion shook the ship and jags of shattered metal flew dangerously.

'Are you all right, sir?'

'Yes.' The Captain reached out to the binnacle for support. His face was as pale as death and there was blood running from his forehead.

'The doctor, sir—'

'No. I shall continue to fight my ship.' Lees-Rimington shook Cameron off and stood straight. Three turrets were still firing, they needed no further orders – he had a first-rate ship's company. They knew what his intentions were. Aboard the German, the fire had spread. The smoke was thick, billowing across the water to lay a heavy pall between the two ships; and now the *Northumberland* was burning too, burning where X turret had been, and her smoke was mingling with that from the enemy. Lees-Rimington looked aft. He gave a sudden exclamation: a body was hanging from a broken davit where a German shell had smashed away a motor-cutter – not so much hanging as impaled like a specimen moth. It was the Commander. Lees-Rimington turned again to Cameron.

'All hands, clear the engine-rooms and boiler-rooms.'

Cameron bent to the voice-pipe. The order was passed down. The engine and boiler spaces were evacuated under the engineer officers, ERAs and Stoker Petty Officers: just in time. The first torpedo hit was now taking further effect; bulkheads were going under the water-pressure and a buckling effect was fracturing steam pipes, producing chaos as the spaces filled with superheated steam. Men fought for the air-locks to get out to comparative safety. Many didn't make it and the comment amongst those who did was bitter: the Captain had left it too bloody late.

From the compass platform Lees-Rimington stared across the sea towards the smoke pall that by now hid the *Helmut Genscher* from sight. The *Northumberland*, with her main deck almost awash, was still firing her last available shells blind into the smoke. The odd shell was still coming back from the German: one came now, slap across the compass platform, accompanied by its wind and a high whistling scream. Cameron ducked instinctively. Lees-Rimington remained standing upright and survived by a miracle. So did the Chief Yeoman of Signals, who had prudently ducked like Cameron. Not so the Navigating Officer, whose body, intact from half-way down the chest, was hurled by the force of the impact up into the air and down into the sea to starboard. The shell went on its way, bringing up a spout of water some four cables'-lengths clear of the ship's side. Then the smoke pall split, forced aside as it were by a tremendous explosion aboard the *Helmut Genscher*. The German could once again be seen clearly, aflame from end to end with one explosion following on the heels of the other.

In a shaking voice the Chief Yeoman said, 'She's going, sir.'

Lees-Rimington nodded. 'Yes. So are we. Cameron?'

'Sir?'

'Abandon ship.'

The tannoy wouldn't penetrate below-decks any more: below-decks was now below water. Men lined the upper deck as the word was passed by the shrilling of the boatswain's calls. Such boats and Carley rafts that could be got away were virtually floated from the davits and other stowages. Some men jumped, without orders, straight into the water and swam in an attempt to get clear before the final rush of water closed over the cruiser as she sank. She was almost on an even keel, and she would go down flat, with maximum suction effect. Before the engine-rooms had been evacuated, the

66

shafts had been stopped: there would be no danger of anyone being churned to bloody fragments of flesh by any thundering screws. That was something to be thankful for.

Lees-Rimington said, 'All right, Cameron. Away you go.'

'I'll stay with you, sir.'

'You have been given an order, Cameron. Kindly obey it.'

Cameron looked at the Captain. The face was haunted, even whiter than before, the features twisted. But he was in command yet. He was suffering badly; no captain liked to lose his ship even when he had sunk his adversary. Cameron said, 'Aye, aye, sir,' and saluted before turning for the ladder. It seemed as though Lees-Rimington intended to go down with his ship – he was of that breed. He hadn't noticed Cameron's salute; he was staring towards the remains of the *Helmut Genscher*, now almost gone. It was likely enough there were no survivors; the many explosions would have ensured that. There were no boats to be seen.

Cameron, reaching the upper deck, made his way aft through a slop of water. Beneath his feet, the bodies of Stripey Barnard and many others wallowed beneath the clipped-down hatches over the magazines. They had been amongst the first to die; the order to flood the after magazines had followed hard upon the blowing-up of X turret. Stripey Barnard and his mates would remain for ever in their steel tomb beneath the South Atlantic. Up top, Cameron found the Paymaster Lieutenant, looking dazed. He said, 'Come on, there's no time to lose now, she'll be gone in a few minutes. Let's grab some hands and get a boat away. It's all we can do.'

Many of the boats had been smashed or burned, including the Captain's galley, but one motor-cutter, two pulling cutters and a whaler got away, plus a number of Carley floats. Heavily overladen with men in every assortment of dress, they pulled and paddled for their lives. Cameron, in the motor-cutter with the Paymaster Lieutenant, took as many as possible of the Carley floats in tow and stood clear. As the boats moved away, hands reached from the water and grabbed for the lifelines along the sides. Cameron took aboard all the men he could without dangerously overloading the boat. One man too many, and all the rest would be in jeopardy. It was a hard decision but a proper and inevitable one and Cameron stood firm by it. They got away just in time: hearing a gush of steam, Cameron looked back. She was settling finally now. There was a roaring sound as the water seethed over the decks and filled such spaces as had not already been waterlogged, displacing air. Great bubbles arose and the sea heaved, dragging at the boats as it rushed to fill the gap made by the sinking cruiser. Cameron looked towards the compass platform: he couldn't see the Captain now, as the water closed over the binnacle. Down she went, the water rising up her masts. She went with her battle ensigns flying, fluttering to the last along a rising wind.

Her disappearance left a feeling of grim isolation. Cameron, who still had his binoculars hanging from the cod-line around his neck, lifted them and studied the boats and rafts in company. He saw gold-braided shoulder-straps on white uniforms, and he cupped his hands and called out.

'Are there any executive officers there?'

'Here,' a voice called from a Carley float. Cameron saw a sub-lieutenant RN – the sub of the gunroom, Harley. 'There are two mids in the cutters. The Commander's gone, so's Number One.'

And so had the Navigating Officer, Cameron knew only too well. He cast off the floats in tow and took the motor-cutter back through the small flotilla, making a rough count of heads. Some one hundred and thirty men had survived. Many were wounded. Of the officers he found the Surgeon Lieutenant, the Paymaster Commander, the Commander(E) and two of his engineer officers, plus Harley and the two midshipmen, these three being the only executive officers. Then to his astonishment he was hailed from one of the Carley floats.

'Mr Cameron, sir!'

He turned towards the voice. 'Yes?'

'Captain's steward, sir. I got the Captain, sir. Would you come alongside and take 'im off, sir, please?'

'Hold on.' Cameron took the motor-cutter ahead and grappled the float alongside. 'Captain, sir,' he said, seeing Lees-Rimington lying flat in the bottom of the float.

Petty Officer Steward Dart said, 'No use, sir. 'E's out cold.'

'What happened?'

'I went to get 'im, sir. Went to the bridge. I knew what 'e meant to do, see. I've been with 'im in three ships, sir. Always asked for me, 'e did. I understood 'im. He's not a bad old b – not a bad gentleman, sir. Tetchy, that's all. I wasn't going to see 'im drown.' Dart sniffed, wiped a hand across his nose, and added, 'Not that 'e knew it, but I promised 'is missus I'd look after 'im and not let 'im do anything daft. I—'

'Yes, but what actually *happened*?' Cameron interrupted impatiently.

'I drew 'im orf one,' Dart said, not looking too happy about it. 'Bang in the kisser. Then 'e 'it 'is 'ead on a stanchion. I reckon 'e may 'ave me court martialled yet. Can someone give me a 'and to get 'im aboard you, sir?'

Cameron himself reached out. Lees-Rimington was man-handled across to the motor-cutter and laid gently on the boards under the after canopy. Dart embarked and sat down beside him. Cameron said, 'We're overloaded, Dart. I can't have that.'

''E's the skipper, sir. An' 'e won't want to be without me 'andy.'

Cameron blew out his cheeks: this was a poser and a nasty one. Dart was right: Lees-Rimington was still the Captain and if Dart was available to tend him now it would be just as well. He looked a sick man, and not just from the well-meant fist of his servant. Also, Dart had risked a lot ... Cameron made up his mind. He chose two men at random. 'You and you. I'm sorry, but there it is. Nip across to the Carley float.'

One was an able seaman, the other a leading supply assistant. The LSA said complainingly, 'It's not right. First come, first served.'

Cameron said evenly, 'I appear to be the senior executive officer after the Captain. It's right if I say it is. Do as you're told unless you want to face a charge of mutiny when we get home.'

The LSA muttered, lifted a bunched fist. Alongside Cameron in the sternsheets was the Petty Officer of the Quarterdeck Division, PO Blaker. Blaker moved for the LSA and grabbed his forearm. 'Do as the officer says and do it at once. *Get*!'

Both men moved. Cameron breathed easy. First hurdle of command over! When, before the war, he'd done time in his father's trawlers one of the skippers had impressed a basic home truth on the owner's young son: always start as you mean to go on.

It was a daunting responsibility. There were, in fact, as Cameron took pains to confirm beyond a doubt, no executive officers senior to him left alive. He got some of the stories: the First Lieutenant had been killed by a shell splinter. The Gunnery Officer and the Torpedo Officer, one a lieutenant-commander and the other a lieutenant, both RN, had died when X turret blew up. An RNR lieutenant, going below with the damage control parties to see what could be done about shoring up a bulkhead after the first torpedo hit, had been caught by a secondary explosion when fire had engulfed some CO_2 containers. No one seemed to know what had happened to the others, apart from the grim sight of the davit-impaled Commander, but the fact remained that until the Captain was fit to take charge, it was all up to Cameron. Circling the flotilla he had been aware of a degree of surliness from Harvey, the RN sub, a short, tubby youth with protuberant eyes. The RN wasn't going to be too happy about being told what to do by the RNVR, and Cameron couldn't help seeing his point of view. The sub had had something like seven years' intensive training, at Dartmouth and with the Fleet. That had to count; but so did the number of stripes and Cameron certainly would not abrogate his new responsibilities. It would be he whom the

Admiralty would hold responsible, and so would the Captain when he recovered. However, it was only sensible to have a natter with Harvey, and he did so, talking across the gap of water. The decision was made to head for Tristan de Cunha, which had been the Captain's aim and which was now the nearest point of land. They could use the boats' compasses, but it would be a hit-and-miss affair, navigating by dead reckoning, with no sextant with which to take sights, and their departure being taken from the last known position of the *Northumberland*.

'Do you know if Father made a situation report?' Harvey asked. 'Did he report by wireless that we were engaging the *Helmut Genscher*?'

Cameron was forced to answer, 'I don't know, Sub. That's to say I don't remember him calling the w/т office. But even if he didn't, I assume the tanker would have made a report before she blew up?'

Harvey said, 'We can't rely on it, can we, for God's sake? You'd better find someone who does remember.'

'I don't think it's important,' Cameron called back.

'Don't you?'

'No. If someone looks for us, well, then, they do – that's all! No way we can influence the chances now.'

'I call that damn stupid.'

Cameron gave an edgy laugh. 'By all means go looking for a telegraphist if you feel the urge, Sub, but don't take too long over it. As for me, I need to watch my fuel tanks. I'm not weaving in and out of the boats and rafts, I'm setting a course direct for Tristan. I'll be relying on you to follow. I'll take the head of the line, you'll take the rear, all right?'

'If you say so.'

Cameron told his coxswain to take the motor-cutter clear, then gave him the course for Tristan de Cunha. Assuming his reckoning was correct, the group of islands lay around eight hundred miles to the south. A long way for small boats and rafts, and no good estimate could be made of their likely speed, which would of necessity be no more than that of the

71

floats under paddle power and the cutters and whaler under oars; in the interest of conserving fuel for the motor-cutter, Cameron, now that it was no longer necessary in order to take the floats clear of the sinking ship in a hurry, had decided not to re-connect the tow. There were all manner of other problems: the chances of being intercepted by another German commerce raider couldn't be discounted, there was the urgent question of food and water, there were the wounded men to be considered, and there was the weather, the sea itself. Currently it was none too kind and looked as though it might worsen.

They headed south, forlorn and lonely in an immensity of water.

7

LEES-RIMINGTON came round: he lifted his head and stared at Cameron. 'Someone struck me,' he said in a slurred voice. 'My servant. Is he here?'

'Yessir,' Dart said. 'Sorry, sir.'

Lees-Rimington shifted his stare. 'Well may you be sorry, Dart.'

'Yessir,' Dart said again, looking uncomfortable. He was a fat man, round and puffy; he was out of his element in an open boat. He was really happy only in the Captain's pantry, *his* pantry where he was king, a place of dishes and napkins, pepper-pots and cutlery. 'I did it for the best, sir.'

'It is never for the best, Dart, to strike one's commanding officer.'

'No, sir. I see that, sir.'

There was a silence but for the sea sounds, the rising wind and the spatter of a cold spray from the wave-tops. The Captain had closed his eyes but Cameron didn't believe he was in anything that could be called a refreshing sleep. His colour was bad and he was breathing heavily. Cameron said, 'I think he's unconscious again.'

'Yessir, so do I. Get the doctor alongside if I was you, sir.' Dart screwed up his eyes. 'Don't like the look of him, that I don't.'

Dr Field would be doing what he could for the wounded men: earlier, Cameron had seen him trying to get something organized so that the worst cases could be made a little more comfortable in the boats rather than rough it in the Carley rafts. The sub-lieutenant had been helping him; Cameron felt that the Captain could wait. He wasn't in pain, nothing like that; he could be just dead tired after so many days and nights on the compass platform. 'We'll hang on a while,' Cameron said.

The flotilla moved on, slowly. As the sun crept past noon Cameron thought about food. The boats' equipment included basic survival rations – biscuits, condensed milk, chocolate, barley sugar; and there was fresh water in the tanks. But the stocks were not sufficient for all the survivors and at a guess they couldn't expect to get by for more than a couple of days. After that, starvation, unless they were able to make a land-fall, and it was manifestly impossible for them to cover eight hundred miles in time. Their speed was not much more than two knots ... say sixteen days. Long before that the men would be too exhausted to row or paddle. There would be no help from the South Atlantic currents: away eastwards was the Benguella Current, but that was heading north; to the west was the Brazil Current. They were between the two. In the early afternoon the wind freshened further, and a spatter of rain started. Soon it was a downpour, dappling the waves, rattling on the motor-cutter's canopy, soaking the huddled men. Also in the early afternoon, soon after the rain started, the Captain opened his eyes and muttered something unintelligible.

Dart said, 'I didn't get that, sir. Beg pardon, sir.' He looked closely at the Captain: there was something funny about the eyes, he thought. He drew the officer's attention to it. 'Kind of rolling about, sir. White showing – see?'

Cameron squatted in front of the Captain and looked closely. 'It's probably to do with the unconsciousness.'

'I'd get the doctor, sir.'

'Wait a moment,' Cameron said. 'He's trying to talk again, I think.' He listened: all the men in the sternsheets listened with him, keeping quiet as the rain lashed and the boat heaved in a twisting motion.

Lees-Rimington said, 'The Chief Quartermaster.'

'Yes, sir?'

'The Chief Quartermaster ... terrible thing to say ... must hold Defaulters, tomorrow morning.'

No one said anything. The Captain's eyes were only half open now but the pupils were just visible beneath the upper lids. Once more there was the funny look. He spoke again, but the words slurred and neither Cameron nor Dart could make sense of them. Then there was a sort of rally and the eyes opened fully and looked directly at Cameron. Lees-Rimington said, 'What I shall do is ... what I shall do is ... what I shall do is ... what I shall do is.' Then he stopped. The eyes remained open and staring; but no more words came.

'I don't like it,' Dart said uneasily. 'Do get the doctor across, sir, please!'

Cameron nodded and glanced at PO Blaker. Blaker said, 'Surgeon Lieutenant's now in the second cutter, sir. Give him a shout, shall I??'

'Yes, please, PO.'

Blaker sent a shout ringing across the water. There was a boat's Aldis but he was no signalman and there might not be a bunting tosser in the doctor's boat to read it. The shout was heard and the cutter began to pull across. The boats touched, the gunwales bumping against fenders put out by the motor-cutter's crew. Looking scared, the Surgeon Lieutenant scrambled across the gap, landing in a heap in the sternsheets. Cameron explained the situation. The doctor felt Lees-Rimington's pulse, then flipped back both eyelids, which had fallen shut again. The Captain seemed to be trying to say something more but couldn't get the words out. The Surgeon Lieutenant lifted an arm; when released, it dropped limply back.

'Well?' Cameron asked.

The doctor sat back on his heels. 'He's had a mild stroke. The speech is affected and there's some loss of movement on the left side.'

'How's he going to make out?'

75

'I can't possibly say, old chap. It's minor and I would certainly expect some recovery. He's had a nasty blow to the head which could have caused it, or helped to cause it.'

Dart said in a low voice, 'Oh, my God.'

'So he can't function?' Cameron asked.

'Positively not, for now anyway. Even if he recovers his speech and full use of his limbs, he'll have to be kept quiet, and warm, and dry.'

Cameron said, 'This is hardly a hospital ward, but we'll do our best, though I don't know about dry. Is there anything else you can do, Doc?'

The young doctor shook his head. 'Not a thing. There never is really. Aspirins help, but I haven't any. Rest and quiet, no worry – that's the only way.'

Rest and quiet and no worry – out here in the restless South Atlantic, in the batter of the wind and rain, with no help for hundreds of miles and no real hope that they could ever make Tristan da Cunha ... Cameron wondered just how much the Captain knew both about his own condition and about the anxieties to be faced. He asked the doctor the question direct; the answer was that no one could say how the Captain's mind might be working. Not for sure; but the chances were that he knew all that was going on and was fully aware of his sudden disability and would as a result be suffering an appalling frustration in not being able to communicate. There was, the doctor said, no point in his remaining aboard; there was simply nothing he could do, and the wounded men needed him more. He scrambled back to the cutter and was pulled clear. Cameron looked down at the Captain, now being tucked in by Dart. Then he looked at the grey sea and the waves rearing on their bow from the south-east.

He said, 'Petty Officer Blaker.'

'Sir?'

'I'm taking over the command formally.'

'Aye, aye, sir.' The weather-beaten flesh around Blaker's eyes screwed up in a sudden smile that made him look like a

76

wizened brown monkey. 'You'll do all right, sir, don't you worry.'

Dart would have made a good nurse. Aghast at what his well-meant action had done, he sat by the Captain, keeping his body warm with his own warmth. Lees-Rimington was wrapped in an oilskin that had been produced from beneath the for'ard canopy by the bowman. It went a little way towards keeping out the water that slopped in over the gunwale, and the rain and spindrift that dripped from the canopy like a continuously leaking gutter. Despite Dart, there wasn't much warmth; oilskins were not warm and the Captain was still in whites, as indeed they all were. He was shivering badly; and the cold grew worse as the sun went down the sky. Whites aboard a cruiser were one thing: out here in an open boat, so close to the sea and the spray and the wind, it was rather different, especially when you were wet through from the start. No hot drinks, either – no cocoa from the great galley urns, now spiralled to the bottom of the sea behind them. It was not until you had been a castaway on the broad oceans that you appreciated the wonderful comfort of a cruiser.

Night came down.

Cameron took a chance and burned navigation lights so as to keep his flotilla homed on to the motor-cutter. It wasn't much of a chance, really. It was safer: if there was shipping around, they might be seen if they had lights burning, and they might just as well be picked up as prisoners-of-war by the enemy, if that was the way it went, as by a friendly or neutral ship. It would be one way home in the long run, the run that would last as long as the war did.

Cameron shared the spells of watch and wakefulness with Blaker, two hours on, two hours off. The hours off were spent trying to find sleep in a slop of water with the motor-cutter bucking like a mule. By dawn hunger was beginning to nag badly and Cameron issued some of the iron rations. Gloomily, Blaker munched a biscuit.

'What I could do to a tiddy oggie, sir,' he said.

'Tiddy oggie?'

'West Country, sir. Cornish pasty. I'm from Guz ... Devonport Division. Out of me natural place I was, seeing the old *Northumberland* was a Pompey ship, but that's the war for you. Everything buggered up. Like us.' Carefully, Blaker sucked up crumbs from the palm of his hand; he had eaten the biscuit with, as it were, a safety-net beneath it so as not to waste anything. He looked down at the Captain, still shivering beneath the oilskin and looking like death. 'Poor bloke,' he said in a low voice. 'What a thing to go and happen at a time like this, eh! My old dad, he had a stroke ... lived the rest of his life as a cabbage. Better for him to go and be done with it, I reckon.'

Cameron fancied he could see the frustration in the Captain's face. His servant had fallen asleep now and was snoring, lying hard up against the Captain, almost using him as a pillow.

Blaker grinned and said, 'Babes in the wood, 'cept there's no leaves. Skipper and piss-pot jerker, what a turn-up for the book!'

They headed on. By Cameron's dead reckoning, they had covered around sixty miles by noon. A drop in the ocean. Hopelessness settled like a black cloud. They couldn't make it, couldn't possibly.

They played word games, guessing games – silly games, to Cameron's urging, since they had to be kept sane by doing something, anything rather than nothing. A vacuum could be highly dangerous. They played I Spy With My Little Eye. Cameron treated it almost as an evolution, a formal exercise, issuing reprimands when someone cheated. When the whole repertoire had been gone through, they sang. Popular tunes: 'Roll Out The Barrel', 'Kiss Me Goodnight, Sergeant-Major', 'Funiculi, Funicula' ... after that, service songs with impolite words. Cameron joined in, in fact led. It put them all in better spirits to bawl out, in company with an officer, the words of Old King Cole, a monarch who was supposed to have had a large retinue of craftsmen:

Now Old King Cole was a merry old soul
And a merry old soul was he;
He called for his wife in the middle of the night
And he called for his jugglers three.
Now every juggler had very fine balls
And very fine balls had he;
Throw your balls in the air said the jugglers
Wake up in the morn with the horn said the huntsmen
Screw away, screw away, screw away said the carpenters
Very merry men are we;
But there's none so fair as can compare
With the boys of the Royal Navee ...

The wind carried the singing down upon the boats and floats astern, and the whole flotilla joined in. All except the men in Sub-Lieutenant Harvey's boat, which was seen to be pulling towards the motor-cutter.

When he was within range Harvey called out, 'Motor-cutter ahoy! I say, I don't think it's quite the thing.'

'What isn't?'

'Those words.'

'Why not?' Cameron called back.

'Well ...' Harvey seemed stumped. 'It's all right at a wardroom party. Not out here, with the Captain present. But perhaps the RNVR doesn't understand that sort of thing.'

'Tripe! I've ordered singing, and singing there will be.' Cameron turned his back, face red with anger at sheer stupidity and straight-stripe rigidity. There were some like that – not all by any means, but he'd struck one of those that were.

At his side, PO Blaker chuckled and said, 'He's thinking of the mermaids, sir.'

Then Cameron had second thoughts: he didn't know, and neither did the doctor evidently, what might be going on in the Captain's mind. Lees-Rimington could be taking it all in; and Lees-Rimington happened to be looking right at him. He certainly wouldn't appreciate the words being bawled out in his presence. That wouldn't be prudery, it would be a concern for discipline and the proper respect for a Captain. Harvey might be right after all. Cameron passed the word for the men to clean it up a bit. There was some tooth-sucking, but they seemed to understand.

Later that day the weather began to moderate and the succeeding night was almost balmy, with soft breezes and a swell left behind by the previous strong wind. It was a little warmer. The Captain seemed neither better nor worse and still shivered. He appeared to be able to eat some broken biscuits and he took some condensed milk, thick and sticky, from Dart's finger. He sucked like a baby. It was very distressing. At the next dawn the Surgeon Lieutenant was pulled alongside the motor-cutter to report that four men had died during the night and had been lowered overboard.

'I expect there'll be more,' he said. He came aboard to take a look at the Captain. He went away again without comment. There was still a long way to go, about seven hundred miles probably, and Cameron began to worry about his fuel tanks. There wasn't much left now and soon it would be a case of paddling with the bottom-boards. It wouldn't affect the speed of the flotilla, since the motor-cutter hadn't in any case been able to go ahead faster than the others, but it would be extra effort for tired, hungry men: the motor-cutter would be very heavy to paddle. Cameron stared almost despairingly into the lightening day. They were all going to die now, it couldn't be avoided. He wondered about some attempt at rescue: Sub-Lieutenant Harvey had followed up his own suggestion of trying to find out if the Captain had sent out a report when he had come under fire, and had called the result across to Cameron the day before: such a signal had indeed been made, according to a leading telegraphist among the survivors. The addressee had been Admiralty repeated C-in-C South Atlantic. This had in fact been the very last signal ever made from the *Northumberland* and it had indicated no more than that the cruiser was engaging the enemy. There was no knowing whether or not it would be acted upon. Almost certainly it

80

would not. In the absence of any further signal the eventual fate of the *Northumberland* would not have been confirmed to the Admiralty and even if it were surmised there would certainly be no ships to spare to hunt for hypothetical survivors. Not unless there was one already handy, and that was another imponderable. The only hope would lie in the possibility that the Admiralty might order any available ships into the area to act as a replacement for the *Northumberland*. There might be information in the Captain's head – he might have been told some of the dispositions during his visit ashore in Freetown, but if he had then all that was locked away.

Now and again as the hours in the motor-cutter passed Lees-Rimington uttered confused sounds in an attempt to speak, but no one could make any sense of it. Writing? The Captain had given no sign with his unaffected arm that he wished to try to write anything down. It was a long shot, but Cameron had felt in his breast pocket for his propelling pencil and PO Blaker had produced a water-stained page torn from a notebook.

Cameron approached the Captain and held out the pencil and paper. He asked, 'Is there anything you'd like to write down, sir?'

There was no response except for a movement of the eyeballs and another attempt at speech. The unaffected arm remained still. Perhaps he simply hadn't the strength. It was no use; Cameron repeated the question, then left it rather than disturb Lees-Rimington further.

At this time there were in fact no British warships readily available in the South Atlantic. The Sierra Leone base at Freetown, headquarters of the South Atlantic Command, had within its jurisdiction a cruiser squadron and a number of armed merchant cruisers, plus some destroyers and smaller escort vessels, for the protection of the vital troop and supply convoys to and from the Middle East via the Cape, and there were some auxiliary naval forces at Simonstown in South Africa; but all these were overstretched. Convoy escorts apart, the White Ensign was not conspicuous in the area of sea where the *Northumberland*'s survivors made their slow progress southward. But the great tracts of ocean held other shipping – and some of it was German. Merchant ships from neutral ports, or ports friendly towards the Third Reich, were to be found heading from the far southern seas for a distant night dash through the English Channel to the Fatherland, or to make for ports in occupied France. The commerce raiders had their attendant store-ships, armament carriers, and tankers with whom they made their rendezvous as required.

One of these was the twin-screw steamer *Bottrop*.

The *Bottrop*'s Master, Captain Erich Schmidt, had been heading for his rendezvous with the *Helmut Genscher* to bring replenishments for her magazines when he had intercepted the raider's urgent, plain-language signal that she was about to founder under British attack and that all her bridge complement had been killed.

This signal had been of much personal concern to Captain Schmidt: the Captain of the *Helmut Genscher* had been Captain Horst Schmidt, his only brother. They had sailed the seas in company since the start of the war. Not long after this signal had been intercepted another had come, addressed to the *Bottrop*, one from the German Naval Commander-in-Chief, Grand-Admiral Raeder himself: the *Bottrop* was to steam north-westward to rendezvous instead with another commerce raider, the *Talca*, whose own supply ship had been sunk by a British submarine operating out of Freetown. By this time Grand-Admiral Raeder had received the news of the *Helmut Genscher* and he had sent an expression of sympathy to Captain Erich Schmidt, which was of course an honour, but this had failed to bring any assuagement of grief or of his bitter hatred for the British. Erich and Horst had been extremely close. Captain Schmidt had sent for his Chief Officer, Klaus Wolf. Schnappes were drunk and the British damned to everlasting hell fire; Herr Hitler was heiled, many times. The *Bottrop* would vicariously avenge the dead through the use of the ammunition below her hatches, ammunition that would be flung across the seas from the iron shards of the *Talca*'s guns to bring destruction to any British ship that she fell in with.

'And,' Captain Schmidt said as he thumped a heavy fist on his desk, 'there are my guns too.' He had two four-inch, one to port, one to starboard, well concealed behind false pieces of superstructure and hinged plating; and there were machine-guns mounted in either wing of his bridge. 'I shall not shrink from using them in my brother's memory.'

Klaus Wolf nodded, but made no comment.

8

THE seas, having quietened, remained flat. The sky cleared and the problems became different: now there was sun, scorching sun that blazed down from a sky that seemed to be a pure metal reflector. Men baked and blistered, unable to find any shelter except beneath the canopies of the motor-cutter itself. Those in the floats and the whaler and the pulling cutters suffered torment. Arms and legs and necks, in many cases chests and backs as well, burned. The salt air made it worse. When anything touched against the exposed flesh it was murder.

The prayers now were for a return to the bad weather. In one of the floats the Chief Gunner's Mate swore in a low monotone and did what most of the others had done: he dived into the sea and laid hold of the lifeline along the side of the float and to hell with any cruising sharks. He wasn't certain whether or not there were sharks in the South Atlantic, but there might be. Make enough kerfuffle and they didn't bother you anyway, so they ought to be in the clear. He waved across to another float, where the Master-at-Arms was sitting like God in a surplice, or that was what it looked like. In fact it was a warrant officers' mess tablecloth that the WOs' steward had brought off with him when the ship went down: it was strange what people snatched up at the last moment. It was still stained with blood: the WOs' mess had been used as one of the emergency dressing stations in action.

'All right, Master?' the Chief Gunner's Mate called.

'No, I'm bloody not.'

'Do the sensible thing. Dive in.'

'No, thank you.'

'Why not?'

There was a pause, then the MAA said briefly, 'Can't bloody swim.'

'Can't swim? Jesus Christ.' That was a funny thing, too: the things you didn't know about a shipmate till something brought them to the fore. It was true a lot of the old-timers couldn't swim, made a point of never learning how, on the principle that if you couldn't swim you'd go down quick and not suffer a long torment if your ship was sunk with all its boats aboard. But he wouldn't have thought the MAA was of that generation. The last few years, of course, new entries had had to pass a swimming test, part of it being to float for three minutes wearing a heavy white duck uniform, for what use three minutes would be in the middle of the hogwash.

Meanwhile the sea was comforting against the sun and was just right in temperature. If you made a big mental effort, and shut your eyes, you could imagine you were in Pompey, swimming off Southsea beach, between the Castle and the South Parade Pier, with the missus and the kids. The Chief Gunner's Mate's wife liked swimming and lying around in the sun on the Southsea pebbles; she had a good figure and liked to show it off. He wondered what she was doing now. Would the sun be shining over Pompey? His thoughts roved over Pompey and the dockyard. Pre-war ... all those battleships and battle-cruisers, aircraft-carriers, the lot. So many of them gone now. The Home Fleet flagship lying at the South Railway jetty, opposite the old Keppel's Head Hotel on the Hard: HMS *Nelson*, all spick and span and larded with bullshit, lovely. The dockyard emptying from the Main Gate and the Unicorn Gate each evening, the dockyard mateys pouring out on their bicycles, thousands of them, and the matloes going ashore from the ships. Uniforms everywhere, except for officers. But you could always tell the naval officers: brown or green pork-pie hat, like as not a blue blazer with the naval crown in gold on the breast pocket, naval tie, always a neatly folded blue burberry raincoat over the left shoulder, walking-stick or – if they were young enough to think it grander – a silver-topped cane in the right hand. They strode from the dockyard with eyes staring right ahead, seeing no one. Lesser people altered course out of their way. They strode as though they owned the place – which, in Pompey, they did in a sense. The civilians didn't count. When this lot was over, the Chief GM felt change might come. He felt it in his bones and he knew he wasn't going to welcome it. He too, as a CPO, had his own importance in the town. He didn't want to lose it. He agreed with the officers: civilians were a lesser breed. The Navy was the Navy, nothing like it anywhere on earth. But now civilians had invaded the Navy.

The Chief Gunner's Mate opened his eyes. Christ. Who would have thought, back in those pre-war days, that he would ever be out here, submerged to the neck, in the hands of the Wavy Navy? As his eyes opened they focussed on the port bow of the flotilla; and he saw what Cameron had just seen also: a smudge on the horizon. A ship, as yet hull-down? Surely; and if so, God alone knew what she might turn out to be.

He let out a yell. Whoever she was, this looked like deliverance from the sea.

As the smudge came nearer and developed into a ship, Cameron's binoculars showed two masts, a single funnel, bridge superstructure amidships, raised poop and fo'c'sle. There were derricks on the masts.

'Merchantman,' he said to PO Blaker. 'I can't identify the ensign yet.'

'Doesn't matter much, does it, sir?'

Cameron laughed edgily. 'I don't know about that!'

'I mean there's sod all we can do about it whoever she is, sir.'

'I suppose that's true. If she's a German ... at least they have a good reputation for treating prisoners decently.'

'They're seamen like us, sir. There's a camaraderie, or so they say.' Blaker hesitated. 'Borrow your glasses, sir, please?'

'Of course.' Cameron handed them over. Blaker focussed and looked. After a couple of minutes he said, 'Jerry. Got the ensign now.'

'Sure?'

'Positive, sir.' Blaker handed back the glasses, and Cameron looked. There was no doubt about it. He lowered the binoculars and glanced down at the Captain, to whom a report could not be made though the instinctive urge to do so was strong. It wouldn't have made any difference, of course; the next step was inevitable and needed no order from the Captain: in a word, surrender. There was no need even to pass instructions to the boats in company. The men would all know the score well enough.

Dart emerged from below the canopy, looking anxious. He said, 'I hope they'll treat the Captain proper, sir.'

Blaker answered that. 'Course they will, Darty, don't you fret.' He repeated his earlier words: 'They're seamen, like us. Remember the *Graf Spee*? All the blokes they put aboard the *Altmark* spoke well of the German skipper.'

'Yes, but the Captain's sick. They won't have a doctor aboard, not in a freighter.'

'We got one, haven't we?'

Dart said restlessly, 'Green as grass, hardly taken any temperatures yet.'

No more was said; they just waited for the German to come up. There was no need to use the Aldis: they'd been seen already. The German was altering towards them. The boats and the Carley rafts had drawn closer together, waiting for the pick-up. Sub-Lieutenant Harvey was now bringing his whaler up towards the motor-cutter.

He called across to Cameron. 'I say ...'

'Yes?'

'We're obviously going to be taken prisoner.'

'Obviously!'

'Do you know anything about International Law in regard to POWs?'

'No. Do you?'

'No. But someone'll have to see to things ... insist on our rights and all that.'

Cameron looked below the canopy at Lawson, the Paymaster Lieutenant: they'd talked a lot the last few days and Lawson had told Cameron he'd been a barrister before the war. 'Pay, how's your International Law?'

'Non-existent really, but I can put up a show of erudition if you like.'

'Thanks. I'll be calling on you.' Cameron grinned across at Harvey. 'We'll cope somehow, Sub!'

'I hope so. The Captain, how is he?'

'Bad.'

'He's not going to like this, you know.'

Cameron disregarded that. Talk about solid: how RN could you get? Going down with your ship was one thing and all honour to those who did. But were you really expected to raise your hat politely when rescue approached, and say no, thanks, if it's all the same to you I'll catch the next one?

Now the German was not far off and they could read her name on the bow: *Bottrop*. This conveyed something to the Leading Telegraphist, who called across: 'She's a supply ship, sir – for the *Helmut Genscher*.'

'Is she indeed?' Cameron cursed inwardly. They were not going to be especially welcome, if the *Bottrop*'s crew were aware their ship had sunk the *Helmut Genscher*. This was unfortunate. The German moved in. Cameron saw the crew lining the decks, staring down. The Master could be seen on the bridge, wearing a gold-rimmed peaked cap and a white uniform. With him was a man like a bull, wearing no cap. There appeared to be an argument in progress.

Captain Schmidt's face was hard as granite. He said, 'I shall steam through them and sink them. I shall churn them with my screws, to pieces.'

88

'That would be foolish, *Herr Kapitan*.'

'It is what I shall do and that is an end of it.' Captain Schmidt turned away and paced the cocoanut matting on the deck of his bridge. His hands were clenched into fists and his heart was thumping like an engine. He was thinking about his brother Horst, his childhood companion, a few years older than him and hence his idol. Horst was dead, slain by the filthy dogs the British. It had come to Captain Schmidt who the men in the boats might be – could be, though he was not in possession of all the facts. He would ask questions before he flung his ship into the boats, and he might find another way. He came back to his Chief Officer's side and called across the water through a megaphone, speaking in good English.

'What ship?'

There was a pause, a consultation perhaps, while the British made up their minds whether or not such a question should properly be answered. Then the answer came from a boat with a motor: 'HMS *Northumberland*.'

'Sunk?'

'Yes.'

'In action?'

'Yes.'

'Against whom, please?'

The British officer who appeared to be in charge called back, 'I'm not required to answer that question, Captain, and I'm not going to.'

'Then I say that it was the *Helmut Genscher*.' Captain Schmidt paused. 'Do you deny this?'

There was no answer. The sun shone down in its blaze of heat. The sea was a blue lake, almost unruffled. The British stared back across the water, waiting for the next move, all their eyes on Captain Schmidt, who would surely not leave them to it. The Germans would behave as gentlemen and never mind the fact that they were bloody Huns, squareheads, Nazi monsters and all the rest – they were seamen, and they understood. In the motor-cutter Cameron fidgeted: what was going on in the German Captain's mind? Should he release the facts – if he didn't do so, would the German be justified in leaving them to it? Just how much information was he supposed, under the Geneva Convention, to give willingly and legally? His understanding was that a prisoner-of-war should give only his name, rank and number or, in the case of the Navy, his ship. Nothing else at all.

'What do you think, Pay?' he asked.

Lawson said, 'You've told him all he needs to know. If I were you, I wouldn't add anything further. But it's up to you. You're the skipper now!' He laughed; his nerves were on edge. They were all suffering nerves. It was almost eerie, to be waiting like this on the slight swell. The German had stopped his engines now, had gone astern to bring his ship up, and was just waiting like themselves. There was more argument on the bridge, high above the little flotilla and its near-exhausted seamen. The sun was torture; the sea was still blue and unruffled. But not unruffled for long. Very suddenly the German Captain moved, darting into his bridge wing. A gun swung, was pointed downwards. There was a sustained stutter; pock-marks came out across the water, bullets smashed into woodwork and metal, spraying the flotilla as Schmidt swung the machine-gun in an arc. It didn't last very long: the bull-shaped officer on the bridge grabbed the Captain and pulled him away from the gun. It spun for a moment on its mounting and then lay still.

There was a silence, broken by the cries of wounded men. In the motor-cutter the Paymaster Lieutenant dangled over the gunwale with his skull shattered. Amidships, the stoker in charge of the boat's engine lay dead. The bullets had swept the rest of the flotilla, killing and maiming. One of the midshipmen was screaming on a continuous high note that tore at the nerves. It was a relief when death came. The other midshipman was also wounded. The Chief Gunner's Mate was cursing loudly and clasping his shoulder. Blood trailed in the water from bodies that had gone overboard. There was a curious look on the Captain's face, as though he understood what was happening: he fixed Cameron with a stare so charged that Cameron felt it before he had met the eye, and looked back into dark pools of intensity, wondering what Lees-Rimington wished to communicate.

Then there was a shout through a megaphone, a shout that cut into the almost stunned state of the survivors.

'You will be picked up. You will co-operate.'

The shout had come from the bull-like man on the bridge; not from the Captain. Cameron licked at his lips, stared round the boats at the men. There were shouts of anger, shouts that advised the Germans to get stuffed, to sod off out of it and leave them alone. The Chief Gunner's Mate called savagely, 'Shower of bastards, sir. We don't want none of it. Someone else'll be along.'

Cameron called back, 'No choice, Chief.' He had seen what was happening aboard the *Bottrop*: the machine-gun had been swung on to them again and this time it was the bull-like man who was behind it. The Jerries couldn't let them get away now, couldn't let them live to tell their story to the world. Such an atrocity, such a total negation of all decency among seamen, would have a devastating effect: it could bring the United States into the war, even. The one way to hush it right up would be to take them all back to the Fatherland. To shoot them up and leave the bodies to float around the South Atlantic in the boats until they were found by a passing neutral or a British convoy would be as incriminating as leaving them alive.

The man on the German's bridge called down again. 'You will come aboard. Ropes will be lowered, and ladders.'

Cameron caught the eye of the Chief Gunner's Mate. He said, 'It's inevitable now. No point in asking to be shot down. We can't fight back.'

The Chief Gunner's Mate gave a slow nod, his face hard and bitter. He thought of Pompey again, and his wife, and the young children. Of one thing he was convinced: he wouldn't see home again whatever happened. The Nazis, once they saw they were beaten as one day they would, they'd snuff their prisoners out rather than go on feeding them and guarding them, wasting precious manpower. It stood out a mile: they were animals. When the end looked near, they would want someone to turn on. He stood up in the Carley float, balancing naturally as a seaman, and cupped his hands. He sent abuse across the gap of water.

'You and your bloody Führer ... that Hitler. One day, the sod's going to get a British bayonet up the arse. He can't last, none of you can, filthy swine.' The voice stopped suddenly as the machine-gun opened again in a short burst. The Chief Gunmen's Mate stood for a moment with his mouth open and his eyes glazing over, then the legs gave way and he collapsed, slowly, his arms dangling, and fell into the water. There was a silence.

'Now you will come aboard,' the German called. 'Do not be foolish.' He grinned. 'For you, the war is over.'

There was difficulty in getting Lees-Rimington aboard. The Germans sent down rope jumping-ladders that dangled and bumped the plates as the *Bottrop* heaved to the ocean swell. Two men, superintended by an anxious Dart, lifted the Captain and tried to get his feet on to the wooden battens held between the two rope sides. It was no good. Dart called up to the deck in a frenzy; there were almost tears in his eyes.

'For Christ's sake! Haven't you got a Neil Robinson bloody stretcher?'

The men tending the ladder took not a blind bit of notice; maybe they didn't understand English, Dart thought, and he certainly had none of their lingo. In the meantime the Jerries were getting impatient under urging from the bridge: it was always dangerous to lie stopped for long, just in case of lurking submarines, though Dart believed it highly unlikely there would be any this far south. Shouts in German came down, their purport unmistakable. One of the naval ratings managed to get Lees-Rimington's right foot on one of the treads, and it stayed there, however uncertainly. That was his unaffected side, but he still didn't seem able to grip with the hand. Dart shook his head in concern: poor old bloke! After a lot more shouting from Dart, accompanied by gestures, a Hun came down the ladder with a rope the end of which he looped around the Captain's chest, under the arms, and hauled taut on a slip knot. Then he climbed back to the deck and lifted a hand and the Captain was heaved up like a sack of potatoes, head and arms lolling as though he were a rag doll. Dart shut his eyes: it wasn't decent, and he might drop off.

But all went well.

Once Lees-Rimington was safely laid on the deck, the wounded men were brought aboard in somewhat similar fashion; and when the embarkation was complete Captain Schmidt gave an order and the telegraphs were pushed over. The *Bottrop* proceeded on passage. The prisoners were assembled in the fore well-deck, under the snouts of the machine-guns and the watchful eyes of two German seamen. When the ship was on course word came down that the Master wished to speak to the senior British naval officer. Cameron was taken to the bridge. Captain Schmidt waited, hands behind his back, short, square and formidable – and coldly angry.

'You sank the *Helmut Genscher*.'

'I have nothing to—'

'You sank the *Helmut Genscher*. I am certain. It is useless to deny. You are swine, you and your men.'

'And you, Captain? You fired on helpless seamen in the water. Is that the act of a human being ... even a German?'

Captain Schmidt took a pace forward. As he did so, two seamen closed in on Cameron from either side. This was obviously rehearsed. As Schmidt's hand lashed out, Cameron was seized and held helpless. Like a snake, the open hand struck, lashing Cameron's face, twice right, twice left. It stung: blood ran from where a heavy ring had cut the flesh. Cameron didn't utter. Schmidt said, breathing heavily, 'Swine, swine, swine! My brother you have killed, the Captain of the *Helmut Genscher*. My brother.'

Cameron said, 'I'm sorry about that, Captain.'

'You have a brother? If you have, then perhaps you understand.'

'I think I do understand. But I also understand the rules of the game,' Cameron said steadily. 'I understand that seamen don't behave the way you have.'

Captain Schmidt scowled. 'You are too young to understand, Englishman. War is war, and Germany is glorious. Your people are decadent.' He turned away and strode up and down his bridge for a while, pompously, arrogantly. Then he came back to Cameron and said on a different note, 'Your Captain, who is sick as I have seen. What is wrong with him?'

'A stroke.'

'Ah. A stroke. A paralysis of mind and body?'

Cameron nodded. 'It's a mild one, but—'

'He is nevertheless rendered useless. I know about such things. I have seen the effects of what you call strokes. You have a doctor?'

'Yes.'

'Your doctor will be permitted to attend. Your Captain looked to me most sick – I was watching.' Schmidt rasped a hand across his cheeks. 'And he is a captain. He will be treated as such. I shall show you that we Germans are persons who accord proper respect. Your Captain will be given my spare cabin, and your doctor may attend him there.'

'Thank you,' Cameron said, much surprised. There was an element of *volte face* in Schmidt's words and manner, but the gesture seemed genuine enough and Cameron appreciated it. He believed that in fact Schmidt, having had his outburst, was ashamed of his violent reactions and wished to make some sort of amends for the grim business of the machine-gunning. Some capital might be made from that. Cameron went on, 'I've a further request to make, Captain.'

The eyes looked back at him shrewdly. 'Yes?'

'The Captain's servant. He's devoted to the Captain, who needs his care – really needs it. May he have access?'

'When this is necessary, yes.'

'It's necessary all the time. Constant attendance.'

94

Schmidt blew out his breath. 'First I shall speak to your doctor. I shall be reasonable in the matter, I promise you. But the good treatment of your Captain also depends on other things – it depends on the behaviour of the rest of your officers and men. Do you understand this?'

'I understand,' Cameron said. Schmidt hadn't really changed all that much. It was clear that Lees-Rimington was to be a kind of hostage, might even remain so in Germany: if the men opened their mouths about the shootings in the water, Lees-Rimington might be the one to suffer wherever he was being held. Another thing became clear, too, within the next few minutes: no privileges were to be accorded the other officers. All the survivors were herded under armed seamen, down into a compartment in the bows of the ship, a space some twenty feet by ten, once a fo'c'sle messroom and sleeping quarters. Bunks were ranged around the bulkheads and there was a table in the centre, its legs clamped to the deck. The three portholes had deadlights clamped down from the outside; or maybe, and more likely, they were welded plates attached at the start of the war for greater strength against gunfire. The place had obviously been designed to hold twenty men; now it was to hold all that were left from the machine-gunning: eighty-three all told, including eight officers – all but Cameron, Harvey and the doctor being from the engine-room and accountant branches – and the remaining midshipman, badly wounded.

Petty Officer Blaker looked around in disbelief. 'Talk about the Black Hole of Calcutta,' he observed. 'This beats the bloody band, this does!'

It did; there was nothing more to be said. Life was going to be murder, especially when the *Bottrop* came north into the tropics. Just before the door was put under clamps, the doctor was called for and taken out. Captain Schmidt wished to speak to him. The rest sorted themselves out as best they could, and a space was cleared for the wounded men, who were going to exist in little short of torture.

The Commander(E), John Ferguson, Chief Engineer and

senior of the non-executive officers, was wedged in a corner with Cameron. He asked, 'What's the next step, I wonder?'

'On our part or theirs, sir?'

'Ours. We'll never survive like this. You'll have to see the Master, Cameron. If you don't, I will!'

Cameron said, 'I suggest leaving it for a time.'

'Don't be obstinate, Cameron.'

'It's not obstinacy, sir. Leave it, and the Germans may see sense. Just now, they aren't in the mood. When they think about it, they'll realize we should be landed in reasonable condition. That's when our chance may come.'

'Chance to do what?'

Cameron said quietly, 'We've not surrendered yet, sir, and as far as I'm concerned we're not going to. It's up to us to fight back when we can. What I'm aiming to do is to get control of the ship. There's enough of us if we play it carefully and don't rush anything. We can even cope with the engines,' he added, glancing at the purple cloth between the Commander(E)'s three gold stripes. 'The worst snag is the Captain.'

The Commander(E) nodded thoughtfully; the *Bottrop* steamed on, lifting and falling to the swell as it passed under her bottom. There was a constant rattle and bang from the spurling pipe as the links of the anchor cable shifted about between the cable locker and the capstan. There was a stench of paint and oil and grease coming in from the boatswain's store: it would not be long before body sweat was added to it. Everyone was cheek by jowl; the bunks would have to be shared and a rota worked out for the shifts. It was a nightmare. The wounded men were suffering, crying out through clenched teeth: they couldn't help it, but the sound nagged. Dart was looking desperate, agonizing over what might be happening to the Captain. Cameron wondered how long he would be able to keep control. For all their sakes, the discipline had to hold.

9

DR FIELD was re-admitted.

'He's quite comfortable,' he reported. 'Better off than he was in the boat, of course. Decent bunk, clean sheets. The trouble is, the Germans are being awkward about giving permission for Dart to go along. It seems there's a Gestapo man aboard and he won't have it.'

Dart overheard this, being all ears when it came to Lees-Rimington. He wanted desperately to help repair the damage he'd caused. He asked, 'Why ever not, sir?'

The Surgeon Lieutenant shrugged. 'Probably just being typical Nazis – bloody awkward! Anyway, they've put a man of their own on. A steward. I think he'll behave properly. If he doesn't, he'll have Captain Schmidt after him. I got the impression Schmidt's remorseful about the gunfire business, but he's upset about his brother, whom he insists we killed. I suppose we did – I'm not excusing him, of course, but as an explanation it holds water. Anyway, I got him talking . . . he's been ordered to rendezvous with another raider, the *Talca*, and transfer ammunition to her at sea before running for Brest. After the rendezvous he'll be picking up an escort somewhere south-west of Finisterre.'

'Anything else?' Cameron asked.

'No. That's the lot that's relevant. The rest was about his brother and what bastards we all are. That, and Heil Hitler. Watch out for Wolf, the Chief Officer. He's a right dyed-in-the-wool Nazi, Party member and all that. I don't think Schmidt is quite so dedicated, other than to Germany itself.'

'You didn't gather what his ETA is – when he expects to pick up his escort?'

Dr Field shook his head. 'No. Do you know something? If this stink keeps up, I'm going to be bloody well seasick.' He was looking green already. Cameron hoped he would manage to hold on to it; there wasn't any room to move away in an emergency.

Many of the officers and men had watches on them, watches that still worked. But for these, they wouldn't have known whether it was night or day – their prison opened on to an alleyway lit by electric light, and no clues were given when food was brought under an armed escort and the door was unclamped. They were fed virtually like dogs, in a number of dishes that had to be passed from hand to hand, and the food itself was of the vilest: sour black bread, largely mouldy, and soup that tasted like beans, with the odd potato floating in it. Water was provided sparingly in an enamel can from which each had to drink in turn, and the can was filthy. Some of the soup contained rat droppings. The first issue was supervised by a gaunt, dark man wearing a white shirt and trousers and with a Nazi armband on his left arm. This man, who turned out to be the Gestapo representative, called for the officer in charge when the meal was finished.

Cameron pushed his way through.

'You are Lieutenant Cameron?'

'Yes.'

'There will be questions.'

'I'll not answer questions,' Cameron said. 'I've already said all I'm going to say, all I'm supposed to say.'

'We will see,' the Gestapo man said. 'Come.' He gestured to two seamen standing behind him. They entered the mess-room and took Cameron's arms. He was led away; he left a silence behind him, an uneasy silence. They all knew that the strong-arm stuff, the thuggery of the Gestapo, was about to begin. If Cameron didn't talk, then the Gestapo might try others. Some wouldn't be able to take it: every man had his breaking-point when it came to the crunch. Not that any of them knew anything vital and maybe it wouldn't really matter much if they did answer questions, but if they did, it would leave them with a nasty taste afterwards, especially when the bloody war was over. *What did you do in the war, daddy? Helped the bloody Gestapo, son.*

Cameron was taken up on deck, into the sunlight and the fresh breeze, a relief from the conditions below. He was taken aft to the midship superstructure and up a series of ladders to the Master's deck below the bridge. He was taken to Captain Schmidt's day-cabin, a comfortable compartment with three large square ports facing forward. There was a settee and three arm-chairs, and good mahogany furnishings. Schmidt sat at a big knee-hole desk, on which his cap reposed, doing some paperwork. He looked up in surprise as the Gestapo entered with Cameron. He frowned; there had been no knock.

'What is this?' he asked, speaking German.

'Interrogation of the officer in charge.' The Gestapo officer tapped a finger on the desk top. 'If you please, Captain.'

'What?'

'The desk. I require it.'

'You do, do you, Leber?'

'If you would be so kind.'

'There are other places. There is—'

'Certainly. But here is the place of authority. I shall not take long.' There was steel in the voice: an order was being given. Schmidt's face was flushed and his frown had deepened, but he got to his feet. The Gestapo was all powerful; his brother Horst had also had to submit to their dictates and had loathed doing so as much as Erich. Horst had been a seaman; so was Erich. Their calling was a cleaner one, open, honest and manly. Captain Schmidt moved across his cabin and stood looking out from one of his ports towards the sea, a better thing to look at than Oberleutnant Leber, who was nothing better than a spy.

Leber started the interrogation, seated now in Schmidt's

99

place. The two seamen stood by, though Cameron's arms were released. He was not offered a seat.

Leber put on a pair of steel-rimmed spectacles and brought a piece of paper from a pocket. This he studied for a moment, then looked up.

'Your ship was the County class cruiser *Northumberland*. I know that she sunk our commerce raider *Helmut Genscher* with the loss of all her crew. Permit me to congratulate you.' Leber glanced across at the stiff figure of Captain Schmidt: Cameron saw the gleam in his eye. A little knifing was being done on Schmidt's feelings. 'This is war, after all. Sometimes one side loses a ship, sometimes another. The best wins these small battles. Your captain against another captain —'

There was an interruption from Schmidt. 'Both ships were sunk, Leber.' He was speaking in English; Cameron assumed this to be for his particular benefit. 'Both ships. There was no victory.'

'The British cruiser,' Leber said smoothly, 'was the more powerful ship. So in fact the victory was German . . . but it was a pity your brother allowed his ship to be lost nevertheless. He had torpedoes, he had aircraft.' Leber turned to Cameron and asked, 'Did the *Helmut Genscher* make use of her aircraft, Lieutenant?'

Cameron glanced at Schmidt, who was scowling. He said, 'I'm not commenting on the action, Oberleutnant Leber. I'm not required to under the Geneva Convention.'

The Gestapo officer made a dismissive gesture. 'So. It is perhaps not important now, the affair is done, the ships are sunk. Now to more pressing matters.' He looked down at his notes once more, then up at Cameron. 'What were the orders for your ship, Lieutenant?'

Cameron shrugged. 'I don't know. I'd not been long in the ship. And I was only a lieutenant, not in my Captain's confidence.'

'You must know where you were bound.'

'No.'

'And what you were to do.'

'No.' It wasn't safe even to answer that; if it was confirmed to the German Naval command that the *Northumberland* was under specific orders to find and sink the *Helmut Genscher*, then other British Admiralty plans, unknown to Cameron, could be affected. One thing impinged upon another in wartime, hence the strict discipline of permitted disclosures.

Leber took off his glasses, polished them slowly and carefully with a handkerchief, then replaced them on a bony, shiny nose. 'So. You will not answer. Soon I think you will. In the meantime let us proceed to other matters, yes?'

'Do what you like,' Cameron answered. 'I'm not answering any questions. That's final.'

'Yes?'

'Yes,' Cameron said.

Leber laughed. 'Such assurance in one so young! It is sad. Sad to have to destroy it.' The tone hardened and he leaned forward. 'There is an older one in the Master's spare cabin. One who also knows the answers that I seek but whose mind has gone. You will speak for him, Lieutenant, you who are the senior surviving officer of the military branch, your Navy's command branch. I wish to know many things. I wish to know the strength and disposition of your ships in the South Atlantic. I wish full information about your base at Freetown – the security and defence, the offensive potential, the orders in general for the troop convoys and for the fast ships independently routed, which in many cases are those carrying troops. I wish to know if your great liners the *Queen Mary* and the *Queen Elizabeth* are expected to pass through the South Atlantic during the next few weeks. These and many other things. It is not just about your ship, you see.'

Cameron knew that the *Queen Elizabeth* had in fact passed through Freetown not long before, crammed to capacity with troops from Australia and New Zealand. He said, 'I'm not answering questions, Oberleutnant Leber.'

Leber's face tightened up. He said acidly, 'You begin to sound like a parrot, such that your stupid sailors bring home from abroad on their shoulders.'

'The Navy's changed a little since those days,' Cameron said.

'Tell me how. Expand, Lieutenant.' Leber got to his feet, smiling genially now. He had seen some kind of a breakthrough evidently, however tenuous. He came round the desk and laid a hand on Cameron's shoulder. 'We shall sit more comfortably, and perhaps Captain Schmidt's schnappes will—'

'I'm not answering any questions.'

'But the schnappes?'

'No schnappes, Oberleutnant Leber.'

Leber's face changed again: the jaws snapped like a rat's, and the eyes showed venom. He said, 'In that case I must alter my methods and my approach, which has been considerate and easy. For the future, no. Do you understand?'

Cameron nodded. 'Yes, I do. Brutality. Typical Gestapo, from what I know of —'

'Propaganda only.'

Cameron laughed in his face. 'Which you're about to disprove!'

'There are occasions when it is necessary.' Leber was in a nasty mood by this time. He said, 'It is necessary now.'

'Do what you like. I can take it.'

'Perhaps. You are an obstinate young man with a foolish idea of what is your duty, of what is brave and what is stupid. Since Germany is winning the war in any case, your attitude is more than stupid, it is unnecessary. However, that is your attitude and I shall accept it.' Leber smiled, a nasty sight. 'Your own pain you might well endure, but not that of another person.'

Cameron's hands clenched. 'Just what do you mean by that?'

Leber smiled again and said, 'Your Captain, the sick man. He will be the one to suffer if you continue to refuse to answer my questions. You will watch, Lieutenant.'

Cameron felt sick: he couldn't watch Lees-Rimington

being manhandled, being made to suffer pain when totally unable to resist. But even if he gave his answers, his small amount of knowledge must certainly fail to satisfy Leber. In growing anxiety he saw Leber beckon to him, then heard him give an order in German to the two guarding seamen, who moved for the door with the Gestapo man behind them: obviously, they were heading for Schmidt's spare cabin. But Schmidt intervened. Swinging away from the port he said, '*Nein.*'

Leber turned round, his face livid. Speaking German Schmidt went on, 'You men, stay where you are. Leber, you will not do this thing.' It was obvious to Cameron, language difficulty or not, what was going on. 'I shall not allow this.'

'I shall do my duty,' Leber said, 'and my duty is—'

'No, Leber!' Schmidt smashed a fist into his palm. 'This is my ship. I am the Master, the Master under God. You—'

'He killed your brother, Captain Schmidt.'

'Yes. My heart does not forgive him for that. My mind does. This is war, Leber.'

'Yet you used your guns against the men in the boats.'

'Yes. I am ashamed of that. My mind was in a turmoil, Leber. It was a terrible thing. But you will not inflict pain on a suffering man, a man who is a captain of the British Navy, a seaman like myself and my brother. If you persist, I shall place you in arrest, Leber, I promise you.' Cameron saw that Schmidt was sweating profusely; rivers ran down his cheeks, dark patches had appeared on his white uniform, but his face was set. However dangerous it might be to oppose the Gestapo, he was not going to weaken. He was the Master, at any rate until the *Bottrop* reached port and Leber sent in his accusations.

Leber read the determination in the formidable face. He had no intention of submitting himself to the indignity of arrest and would not take the chance of the crew remaining loyal to their Captain rather than to the Party. That could well happen: Leber was under no illusions; seamen were a race apart. He shrugged and said, 'Very well, for now you are certainly in command of the ship, Captain Schmidt, and I must of course consider myself under your orders. I submit, as it were, to *force majeure*. There are other avenues yet to be explored.'

Cameron was taken back to the messroom in the bows, back to the smells and the crush. Leber went with him, as did the escort. Leber was humming a tune, putting a brave face on his vanquishment by Captain Schmidt, but his face was twisted with evil. There was, he said, an officer with purple cloth between his stripes, an engineer. Not of the command branch, but a much older man than Cameron. As head of the engine-room complement, he would be in his Captain's confidence in regard to a number of things that might be helpful to the Third Reich. Cameron did what he could to deflect Leber, but without result.

The Commander(E) was called out and taken away.

Cameron told the rest of the men, briefly, what had happened in the day-cabin. They took it in silence but the atmosphere was tense. Cameron reflected on engineers. The Chief, as the Commander(E) was usually known in the ward-room, would indeed be in possession of certain information. He had the responsibility of ensuring that he had oil fuel enough to arrive at the destinations ordered by the Captain and of anticipating his future requirements for bunkers, thus he would have to know that destination and the planned route to be taken. Insofar as his engine-room was concerned he would have to know the repair capacities of British bases such as Freetown, and the work-load progress on other ships in the river. He would have some knowledge of the convoy pattern and of the ahead movements of shipping. And many other things that Oberleutnant Leber could pass on to the relevant quarters and thus complete a jigsaw. Captain Schmidt might do his best to inhibit brutality if he knew it was happening, but Schmidt was in something of a cleft stick and having stuck his head out in regard to Lees-Rimington might hesitate, after due reflection, to stick it out again for a man who was not sick. After all, Leber knew all about that machine-gunning ...

Time passed. The conditions in the messroom were already intolerable, and so far they had been incarcerated for a matter of hours only. So many days yet to go: sickness would strike unless they were permitted exercise. It would be up to himself, Cameron knew, to make representations on that point. He could scarcely breathe, so little room was there. Bodies pressed into each other. Next to Cameron was PO Blaker, who, with Sub-Lieutenant Harvey, had already drawn up a list of bunk sharers, in shifts. The period each man spent in the bunks would be the one respite. The days would be grim. Blaker tried to be cheerful, having taken note of the officer's gloomy face. Depression, too much depression, could be fatal. They mustn't sink into despair.

Blaker said, 'What price Pompey now, sir?'

'Priceless!' Cameron said.

'We'll see it again. All that beer, cor! Won't see me for dust, slap bang through the gates at RNB and into Queen Street. Lovely pubs, sir. Lovely women, too.'

'I thought you were a married man, Blaker?'

'I am, sir, so not a word to the missus.'

Cameron grinned. 'I'm surprised at you!'

'I'm surprised at meself an' all, sir. Sailors are a bloody rotten lot. I wonder any woman ever marries any of us.' Blaker paused. He was nattering away just to keep lively, really, and nonsense was as good as anything else that came to mind. 'You married, are you, sir?'

'No.'

'Lucky for some! Bit o' skirt, sir?'

'You could say so. A leading Wren at RNB as it so happens.'

'Oh yes, sir. Whereabouts in the barracks?'

'Drafting Office. Mary Anstey.'

Blaker let out a long whistle. 'Well, I'll be buggered! Talk about a small world.'

'You know her?'

'Handed me the bloody draft chit that sent me to the old *Northumberland*, sir. With 'er own lilywhite 'and, she did.' Blaker ruminated, staring wide-eyed into such space as was available. 'Sorry about the bit o' skirt, sir. It doesn't fit her. Not the sort you'd say that of. A very nice young lady, sir, is Leading Wren Anstey, and I offer you my congratulations and hope you'll be very happy.'

'Thanks, but don't jump the gun,' Cameron said sardonically. 'No final decisions yet.' The phrase jump the gun brought to mind a story about a Master-at-Arms who was to be best man at a wedding. The Master-at-Arms, deeply dyed in naval routine and the defaulter's table, spent the night before the ceremony in close study of the marriage service and attendant regulations. Next day, the bride came up the aisle some six months pregnant. Came the moment when the parson said, 'I now pronounce you man and wife.' The Master-at-Arms emerged from a reverie and barked: 'Granted, back-dated six months, salute the Captain, 'bout turn . . .' Cameron found himself smiling; Blaker saw his face and decided he'd achieved his objective. It didn't last, though. A minute or so later the Commander(E) came back. Or was more strictly thrown back. The clamps came off the door and a trembling body was heaved through with its white uniform torn and bloodied, its gold-and-purple shoulder-straps hanging loose down the arms.

The Commander(E) was picked up by two ratings and carried through the crush and laid in a bunk. He had two black eyes and a broken nose and there was heavy bruising all over, but he was fully conscious. He swore without stopping for a good two minutes. Then he said in a hard voice, 'Go on, someone. Ask me if I told the bastard anything.'

Cameron said quietly, 'I wouldn't presume to ask that, sir.'

'Thanks for your confidence, Cameron. Well, I'll answer it anyway: did I buggery! But I put over a bloody good line of bull at the end. I just hope it was convincing, but I may get bowled out. Time will tell, I suppose. I told Leber that Admiral Tovey with the Home Fleet was under orders to seal off the Channel approaches right across from Biscay to the Lizard and sink all returning commerce raiders and their supply ships. Which means, if he believes it, that Schmidt will have either to attempt to reach his Fatherland north about, which will bring him slap into the range of our shore-based aircraft and the fleet units from the Clyde and the Forth, and Scapa ... or he'll have to hang about in the South Atlantic till he's forced to enter a port somewhere to replenish his bunkers.' The Commander(E) paused. 'I think it gives us a little leeway.'

Cameron said, 'Yes, it does,' but he was not too happy as to the possibilities if Schmidt should decide to go well out into the North Atlantic and then risk turning east across the north of Scotland. To be bombed or shot at by their own side would be somewhat final, considering the cargo that was known to lie beneath the *Bottrop*'s hatches. After all, she was an armament supply ship.

That afternoon Lees-Rimington's condition apparently gave Captain Schmidt cause for alarm. The Surgeon Lieutenant was sent for and taken to the spare cabin under guard. He was away for some time but when he was brought back he looked reasonably optimistic. He said, 'I played along with Schmidt's anxiety ... there's no change really, but I've managed to get permission for Dart to go along and replace the German steward.'

Dart went off right away, being taken over by the armed guard. The rest grew more and more morose. By now they were accustomed to the various smells: noses had become anaesthetized. But the overcrowding was different; it wouldn't go away and its effect worsened. Even a destroyer's messdecks had never been like this. The sub, Harvey, was suffering badly. Dartmouth hadn't prepared him for such conditions, tough as life had been in other ways. He was panting for breath, and not just from the closeness of the atmosphere: it was a kind of incipient panic, Cameron thought. He had a word with Dr Field, who pushed through

107

the mass of men and wedged himself alongside Harvey and began a conversation, anything to take the sub's mind off himself. If an officer should crack now, the effect would be grim. The doctor talked about his days as a medical student, not so far behind him, and told some anecdotes about the weird cases that came to casualty: stories mostly of sexual deviants or cack-handed probationer nurses – cack-handed medical students too. Once, not in casualty but on a ward, a probationer had been told by Sister that a certain patient was not to leave his bed to use his commode: the patient's head was subsequently seen over the top of the screen, where he was seated on the commode placed on the bed.

Harvey didn't seem to think it funny; in fact he was scarcely listening. There was nothing the doctor could do but go on talking, but he couldn't keep it up for ever. He had other worries: the wounded, lying in the bunks. He had managed to persuade Schmidt that the contents of the ship's medical chest should be made available but when he had examined it he had found little that would be useful. It was like any ship's medicine chest, he assumed: plenty of laxatives, plus a number of antiseptics and lotions for the emergency treatment of venereal diseases. He equipped himself with some bandages and with some bottles of TCP. What he really wanted was morphine, but there was none available. So they all had to listen to the sounds from restless, pain-racked men.

Cameron spoke to Petty Officer Blaker. 'How many do you reckon in the crew?' he asked.

'Forty, sir, give or take a few. Forty, all hands.'

'We've got more than enough, then.'

'To take over, sir?'

'Yes, and to steam the ship afterwards. There are ERAS and stokers, and the engineer officers. Mr Harvey and myself on the bridge.'

'Yes, sir. No guns, though!'

Cameron nodded. 'We'll just have to manage without till we can grab some from the crew.'

108

'When are you thinking of doing it?' Blaker asked. 'We don't get a lot of chance, do we?'

Cameron said, 'When they bring the meals.'

'They'll be ready for that, sir.'

'I know. But it's the only chance I can see. If you've any better idea, let's have it.'

Blaker hadn't. Meal times were the only contact with the German crew, other than when the Surgeon Lieutenant was sent for and there was a hesitation about using Dr Field as a kind of Trojan horse: if the attack should miscarry, they might take it out on the doctor insofar as future visits to Lees-Rimington might be forbidden, and then the Captain would be the chief sufferer. Cameron wouldn't risk that, nor would Blaker.

10

BY this time the Admiralty in London had made such dispositions as were possible, following upon the news that the *Northumberland* had been in action with the *Helmut Genscher*. The absence of further signals could mean simply that the *Northumberland*'s Commanding Officer had decided not to break wireless silence again if he had sunk the enemy ship; but on the other hand silence could indicate a tragedy for Britain. Just in case, signals were encyphered and sent urgently to the Commodores of the convoys passing by the area and to the Senior Officers of the escorts, warning them to be on the lookout for boats. Not much hope was entertained for survivors if indeed the *Northumberland* or the *Helmut Genscher*, or both, had gone down; and, having done what they could, the operations room staff concentrated their energies on the business of seeking out the remaining German commerce raiders known to be still at large in the South Atlantic, one of them being the *Talca*. At this time Admiral Sir John Tovey was in Scapa Flow with his Home Fleet flagship HMS *King George V*; he was ordered to detach two cruisers to head south from Scottish waters to carry out what might well be a totally fruitless search.

It was a wide canvas.

The cruisers would carry out their search independently of each other, one heading on a course to cover the eastern part of the great ocean on the African side, the other to move westwards towards South America and Cape Horn. There was far too much sea-room in between. As the orders went out a bulky figure was present, smoking a cigar and looking sombre, brooding.

He said, 'Useless in my view, Admiral. But don't let me interfere.'

'It's all we can do, sir.'

'I know, I know.' The cigar was waved in the air, tetchily. 'It's ships we need desperately. Ships, ships and more damn ships. We're hamstrung as it is. We should have re-armed sooner. I was always saying so, if you remember!' Suddenly a twinkle came into his eyes. 'Perhaps I protested a little too much. Whatever it was, no one took any notice of me – not then. Now it's almost too late. Almost. Not quite. We shall succeed, we shall conquer.' The brooding look returned. 'Those two cruisers ... some hope!'

The Admiral said, 'They're modern construction, sir. They have RDF. That should help.'

'Fiddlesticks!' The heavy shoulders hunched. 'What I understand the Americans call radar ... range of a few miserable miles. Oh, I don't denigrate the thing, it's useful enough for air defence. But have you any idea how *large* the South Atlantic is?'

The Admiral smiled pacifically. 'I have some inkling, sir.' The bulky man got to his feet; he had to return to the House. An all night sitting most probably, he said, and he'd dearly love to have some good news come through before the House rose. Too much depression wasn't good for the country. The Navy must produce more sinkings. So much of the past heroism had been in lost causes.

Next day the *Bottrop* moved into bad weather: high seas, with high winds to drive them aboard the freighter's decks where they swept in thunder and spray above the hatch covers to surge away through the wash-ports. Life in the fo'c'sle messroom became more uncomfortable and more noisy. The seas crashed down overhead and the spurling pipe set up a continual roar and rattle as the cable was flung about in its metal tube. The din was appalling and the ship's motion horrible;

111

the air was foetid by now, and was worsened as men vomited. The messroom rose in a series of stomach-wrenching jerks, remained poised for a moment, then came down again with a rush ... another brief pause then the whole thing started again. Leaks developed, and soon the deck was awash, the water swilling from side to side on the roll and end to end on the pitch. It was the worst corkscrew motion Cameron had ever endured: the trawlers of his father's fishing fleet had been bad enough, but the movement had been sharper and shorter; this was murder. Also, the living quarters in the trawlers had been comparatively clean; by now the messroom was filthy and it was unlikely it would be hosed down and swabbed out for the rest of the voyage.

During the afternoon two of the wounded men died. One was the nineteen-year-old midshipman, the other a three-badge stoker first class. Each end of the scale, age-wise. The stoker had been a busy man in his time: eight children, according to a Stoker Petty Officer, and another on the way. He must have done more than his share of home service. 'Or the other way round,' the Stoker PO said reflectively. 'Between foreign commissions, like, sir. Absence makes the 'eart grow fonder and the pr—'

'Yes, quite,' Cameron interrupted: he felt the occasion to be not one for lower deck humour even though such often enough relieved tension.

'Poor old Shorty,' the Stoker PO went on, not to be denied his requiem. 'Should by rights 'ave bin called Everard...'

It wasn't disrespect for the dead, far from it: more like deference. Cameron had a word with the Surgeon Lieutenant, who was looking sick at his inability to do his job to his satisfaction. Both men, he said bitterly, had died in agony from severe stomach wounds. And they had been casualties from the *Bottrop*'s machine-guns rather than from the action against the *Helmut Genscher*, which made it all the worse.

'Water under the bridge,' Cameron said. It would be fatal to allow introspection, to let things get on top of them. 'Now the bodies have to be disposed of. Will you see Schmidt, or shall I?'

'You,' the doctor answered. 'I've seen enough of him, thank you!'

Cameron pushed through and banged on the steel door with a bunk-board. He banged for some time but nothing happened: that might prove one thing – that the door was unguarded except when it was opened for meals. It might be worth bearing in mind, though how one got through a clipped-down steel door Cameron knew not. He stopped his banging; no one was going to come along. Harvey was staring at the body of the midshipman, over which someone had draped a shroud of a couple of seamen's 'flannels', a garment like a collarless and buttonless shirt worn by ratings in bell-bottom rig. It had an undignified and almost apologetic aspect, as though it knew it would give offence unless moved out. Harvey was looking green but appeared not to be able to look away; he had been sub of the gunroom, a fairly exalted position that allowed him to cane warts for real or imaginary offences against gunroom etiquette or for lapses in good seamanship. He and this dead wart had lived in close proximity aboard the *Northumberland*. Cameron made his way across and said, 'Don't brood, sub. It doesn't help. We're going to come through.'

'The mid isn't.'

'I know. Same applies to a lot of others. We've just got to take it, that's all.'

'Can't he be moved? It's bloody awful, just—'

'I know,' Cameron said again. 'I'll see to it as soon as someone opens up.' Harvey lifted his hands and put them over his face. His whole body trembled and Cameron heard sobs. A shaft of anger entered him and took over. Harvey was an officer and had a responsibility to the ratings: officers couldn't go to pieces however bad they felt. Cameron had learned that in the trawlers; skippers and mates who'd been sick or injured but had kept going because they and they alone had the knowledge and authority to bring the boat safe home to harbour. Being an officer was not just wearing a bit of gold braid and impressing the girls ashore. Cameron reached out and pulled the hands clear of the face, then shook the sub's body till his teeth rattled.

'Pull yourself together sharpish,' he said in a low voice. 'Don't act like a woman. There are *men* watching.'

Harvey's face went a deep red. He said, 'You bastard. What does the bloody RNVR know?'

Cameron grinned and let go. He'd done a bit of good, even if it didn't last. It would be something if the RN merely felt a need to show up the RNVR.

No one came to the messroom until it was time for the next meal. Then it was the usual procession, two cooks with the foul food and some water, plus two armed guards. Cameron said he must see the Master and explained why. He was told to wait; when the food had been shoved in the Germans clipped down the door again and went away. Ten minutes later Cameron was removed and taken to see Schmidt in his day-cabin. He appreciated the fresh air, even the soaking he got from the water flinging down from the fo'c'sle-head as he grappled his way along a lifeline rigged from the break of the fo'c'sle to the foot of the midship superstructure. It gave him a rudimentary wash.

Schmidt said, 'I am sorry about the deaths, Lieutenant. You wish to discuss their disposal, I think.'

'Yes.'

'They will be committed to the sea. It will be done properly. They will even have a White Ensign.'

Cameron nodded. The German would have many naval ensigns to be hoisted as appropriate for fooling a British ship if they should encounter one. That was routine. He said, 'I have a request, Captain.'

'So?'

'British ratings, killed in action ... they should have their own ship's company present. I'm asking permission for some of us to attend.'

'Who, then?'

114

'Myself, Sub-Lieutenant Harvey, the Commander(E), and some of the stoker's messmates.'

'Yes. A reasonable request, perhaps. As a seaman, I understand. Of course I understand. This I shall consider and will let you know. But there is something else: as a seaman you will understand that the committal cannot be made in such weather as we are now going through. The wind and sea come from dead ahead and I cannot make a lee without altering my course. If I alter my course, I shall bring the weight of the sea broadside and will be in much danger of broaching-to.'

'I don't think the seas are that bad, Captain Schmidt.'

'No? I do. I am a man of many more years than you, and more experience. I shall not hazard my ship. Nor shall I hazard the bodies.' Schmidt grinned and went on, 'According to the pastors, the dead will rise again. Maybe they will. But they must not come back aboard the *Bottrop*.'

Cameron had to be content with that, though he suspected that Schmidt was merely procrastinating: very probably he had to get approval from Leber before he could permit a British presence on deck. In the meantime, Schmidt said, the bodies would be removed from the messroom and taken good care of. Cameron was escorted back to the messroom, where he reported to the Commander(E).

Ferguson asked, 'What are the chances of the Gestapo man agreeing, d'you suppose?'

Cameron shrugged. 'Your guess is as good as mine, sir, but old Schmidt isn't the sort to be sat on too hard. I believe he may win out. If he does, we could say our time has come – don't you think?'

'To attack, d'you mean?'

'It's as good a hope as trying to nab the meal-time guards,' Cameron pointed out. 'There'll be several of us out there on deck. Of course, there'll be a strong Jerry mob—'

'Right, there will! That's the snag, surely?'

'It could be, but it could act for us rather than against us. They'll be in a handy bunch, a sort of crew muster. If we can

115

disarm them in a group and turn their guns on their mates on watch, we'll have a pretty fair chance of seizing the ship. I think it's worth bearing in mind.'

Half a dozen of the crew came down to take away the bodies; they would not enter the messroom but demanded that the dead be passed through to them. After that, there was a long wait. Cameron used the time to formulate a plan for attack in the event of permission being given for some of the prisoners to attend the committal. He assumed that the Gestapo man, Leber, would attend as well as Schmidt. He was hopeful that in addition to himself he could get approval for six British to be present, four of them being stokers, messmates of the dead engine-room rating. The Commander(E) would detail four hefty men as potential mourners. He was not small himself: he had boxed for the Navy and he was keen to hit back at the Germans who had beaten him up. Cameron's plan was that as the bodies slid from the plank, two stokers would attack Schmidt and the other two would attack Leber; Leber would be armed for sure. His gun would be taken and used to cover the rest of the crew. The Commander(E), Harvey and Cameron would go straight into the armed seamen nearest to them and gain control of their rifles. Everything would depend on sheer speed. Once they had the Germans in their gun-sights, Harvey would double below and release the rest of the prisoners.

Cameron said, 'The bridge is going to be the big snag. The machine-guns—'

'They'll be turned on us right away,' the Commander(E) said.

'Yes, sir. We've got to get them first, that's all.'

'You mean, shoot down the bridge personnel?'

'No option, sir. It can be tricky – it may mean leaving the wheel without a helmsman, and the ship could come broadside, but—'

'Worse than that,' Ferguson broke in with a hard laugh. 'If this doesn't come off, we'll all have had it. Killing the guards

116

whilst prisoners-of-war isn't very kindly looked upon to the best of my knowledge and belief!'

'It's the only way,' Cameron said. 'We just have to bring it off, that's all. It's all or nothing.'

'I supposed you've weighed the pros and cons, Cameron?'

'I have, sir.'

'What I mean is this.' The Engineer Officer's face was serious. 'Is it going to be worth risking the lives of all the survivors? What, in hard fact, do we stand to gain – apart from one German supply ship, always assuming we're able to bring her to a British port? I'm pretty sure Schmidt will use us as an excuse to shoot down the lot if we fail – and at best it's a fifty-fifty chance, isn't it?'

Cameron nodded. 'That's true. But I aim to get more than the *Bottrop*. If we can gain control, we've a rendezvous to keep!'

'The *Talca*?'

'Yes. I'll keep that rendezvous – the position's bound to be marked on the chart.' Cameron paused, running his glance over the tensely waiting survivors. 'If we get control, we'll have the *Bottrop*'s guns. Perhaps it's a long shot, but at least it's better than spending the rest of the war in a POW camp.'

The Commanding(E) was heard to mutter something about suicide and young idiots who thought they were Nelson. Nevertheless, there was hope in the air now. Inactivity was bad, and they all knew they would outnumber the Jerries by something like two to one as soon as they could double out from the messroom.

Petty Officer Blaker circulated, giving words of cheer; some amongst the survivors didn't go much on being fodder for another Nelson. In the event of failure either they would be shot or they would enter bloody Germany with the established reputation of guard killers and would face a more rigorous imprisonment as a result. The Gestapo would show no mercy. Blaker didn't envisage failure and said so; the Navy would win through. They always had and always would. To the hangers-back this was Nelson again ... and with all due respect Nelson tended to loom a little over-large in the RN. He had been turned into what in his lifetime he had never been: the arch apostle of bull and tradition. Ask anybody in the Andrew why such and such a thing was done, and the answer was invariably 'because Nelson did it'. There never had been another Nelson though plenty of officers fancied themselves in the role. Glory-seekers ... they should be stood well clear of! All the same, there was a grudging acknowledgement even among the bolshies and the doubters that every POW had the duty placed upon him of doing his best to escape. It was all laid down in the Articles of War or somewhere.

Blaker reported back to Cameron in a whisper. 'They'll be all right, sir.'

'Full support?'

'Near as makes no difference. I'll be there, sir.'

Cameron grinned. He knew precisely what Blaker meant: the PO could be a formidable and angry sheepdog. They waited a little longer in a very tense atmosphere and then Captain Schmidt came down himself and the door was opened up. Schmidt said, 'Lieutenant, the weather is worsening ahead. The committal must be soon – in fifteen minutes' time, or it will become impossible. Even now it will be difficult, as I have said, but we must do it.'

Cameron nodded. He asked, 'Have I your permission to attend with a party of six men?'

'Six?' Schmidt pursed his lips, then nodded his assent. 'Yes, you have the permission, Lieutenant.'

'Thank you,' Cameron said.

'We are seamen, you and I. We understand respect.' Schmidt turned heavily away. The door was clipped shut again.

11

THE quarter-hour passed, very slowly: the atmosphere in the messroom was almost electric. The ship was still being thrown about, lifting and falling again, rolling heavily. The moment of tilting the plank would have to be carefully judged by Captain Schmidt unless there was to be indignity.

'All right, sir?' Blaker asked, watching Cameron's face.

'Yes.'

'Wish I was coming with you, sir.'

Cameron grinned. 'To hold my hand?'

'You don't need that, sir.'

'I hope you're right. Anyway, you'll be up soon enough if it goes off as expected. First thing for you to do will be to get to the bridge and get a man on the wheel.'

'All organized, sir.'

'I thought somehow it would be, PO.'

'Mutual confidence, sir, that's the ticket, eh?'

They heard footsteps coming along the alleyway. The door opened as the clips were knocked back. The British committal party had been mustered just inside the door. Now they emerged, to be taken over by the armed Germans, three of them with rifles. They went out into the fore well-deck, into cold and wet, with the heavy seas racing close along the sides. Schmidt had in fact altered a little to the westward in order to provide some sort of lee consistent with ship safety. The engines were still at full ahead by the feel of the ship. It was customary, as a mark of respect for the dead, to stop engines during a committal, but in fact a stopped ship rode worse in a seaway. The sky was heavily overcast and threatening, a gloomy backdrop for the proceedings. From the bridge the Chief Officer looked down, bulking above the guardrail, his face sour. That face clearly said that Schmidt was an old fool, a sentimentalist from the past. The British were pigs and soon Herr Hitler would rule the world.

Two planks were laid side by side on the port rail of the well-deck, covered with a single White Ensign. At the head of the planks Schmidt stood, smart in his gold-braided uniform and peaked cap. Leber was with him, in Gestapo uniform complete with swastika armband. Schmidt carried a prayer book. At each side of the planks stood German seamen, three to a side, to tilt the planks when the order came. Behind, standing on top of the hatch cover, was a posse of armed men. They had the aspect of a funeral firing-party rather than a guard but clearly they could change their role at the drop of a hat.

Schmidt confirmed the firing-party as such. He said, 'It will be done properly as promised.' Cameron gave him a word of thanks. It was not customary, at any rate in the British Navy, to provide a firing-party aboard ship; but Cameron believed Schmidt might be making amends, so far as he was able, for the machine-gunning of the lifeboats. He caught the eye of the Commander(E) and tried to telepathize a message. The Engineer Officer almost imperceptibly closed one lid. Perhaps, with luck, he'd understood: when the firing-party went into their salute – that would be the best moment. Lifted rifles, aimed into the air. There was the hope of a second or two at any rate.

As Schmidt started reading the service Cameron glanced up at the bridge. The Chief Officer, Wolf, had moved to the port-side machine-gun.

Hope receded, but did not entirely fade: British and German would be mixed in the line of fire and Wolf wouldn't want to kill Leber. There was a moral in that: keep close to Leber! The service proceeded. Schmidt read it in German

120

even though his English was good, and Cameron was unable to follow it. But the physical motions were plain enough. When Schmidt closed his prayer book and brought his right hand to the salute Cameron tensed ready to move like lightning.

Schmidt gave the final order, and the planks were tilted. On the hatch cover, the armed men lifted their rifles high.

As the bodies slid, the British party moved as detailed. Two big stokers ran for Leber, twisted his arms up and grabbed his revolver from its holster. Two more pinioned Schmidt. In the same instant Cameron with Harvey and the Commander(E) leaped on to the hatch. From the port side of the bridge the machine-gun twisted, trying to find a clear bearing. Cameron wrenched one of the rifles free, then used its butt as a club and laid into the other Germans. Harvey, obeying orders, had made his dash for the fo'c'sle alleyway. The machine-gun opened; lead spattered against the fo'c'sle bulkhead but Harvey made it into the safety of the alleyway. Ferguson was not so lucky: a chance bullet took him in the throat and he went down, choking in his own welling blood. One of Leber's captors had the German's revolver rammed into its late owner's back and was shouting at the erstwhile plank-tilters. He was shouting in English but they understood and so did Leber: Leber would have his backbone blown right through his gut if anyone made a move. And Leber was howling for mercy.

Cameron looked up at the bridge: the machine-gun had stopped firing. Wolf was no longer to be seen; somewhere along the line a miracle had happened. By now Harvey had unclipped the messroom door and the whole of the survivors were pouring out, waving bunk boards and all set to smash into the German crew.

It was all but over.

Cameron reached the bridge ahead of the able-seaman detailed to take over the wheel; and he found Dart behind the machine-gun. Dart, obviously the miracle, was covering the wheelhouse with the snout and all ready to press the button if anyone amongst the bridge personnel should move for the starboard gun.

Cameron said, 'Dart, you're a bloody wonder!'

'Quite all right, sir. Just did my duty, sir.'

'Might one ask how?' There was something about Dart's portly manner that made one formal and dignified.

'Yes, sir. When I 'eard the shooting, I come up to the bridge pronto, being worried about the skipper like. And there's this knife, sir, see, on a lanyard, looped around a stanchion. No trouble – all the bridge personnel, sir, they 'ad their eyes facing for'ard like a lot of dummies.' Dart wiped a hand across his forehead. 'Well, there's the knife, sir, and there's that Chief Officer, be'ind the gun. He's over there now, sir.'

Dart pointed through the half-open door of the wheelhouse.

Just inside, Wolf was lying on his stomach, obviously dead, and the haft of the knife was sticking out from his back. Cameron said, 'Well done! You saved our bacon. What about the Captain?' he added.

'As before, sir, no change.'

'Better go down and stand by him,' Cameron said. 'We haven't accounted for all the Jerries yet. I'll take charge here.'

Dart turned away for the port ladder down to the Master's deck. Up the starboard ladder came Captain Schmidt under guard of two British seamen. His face was livid. He had been let down, he said. His decency had been turned against him. It was dastardly.

Cameron apologized but said, 'I have my duty too, Captain Schmidt. Now *you* will be properly treated. You will be held under guard, but in your own cabin.'

'It is so knavish.'

'I'm sorry.'

When the bridge had been taken over Cameron went down to have a look at Lees-Rimington. He found him sleeping. Dart was sitting by the side of the bunk; he got to his feet when

Cameron came in but was motioned to sit again. He said, 'He's very poorly, sir. That bloody Hun steward didn't help much. Will the Surgeon Lieutenant be up, sir?'

'I expect so, when he's made the other casualties comfortable.'

'Yes, sir, he'll have his work cut out, that I do know.' The steward brought out a handkerchief and blew his nose. 'I'd like to get the Captain back to the Clyde, sir. Just to see his missus again ... she's staying up there, sir, in Rothesay. Victoria Hotel.'

'If anyone can do that,' Cameron said, 'you will.' He left the cabin, his thoughts bleak. Making his way down to the boat deck with the intention of familiarizing himself with the *Bottrop*'s gear and layout he met Dr Field. He said, 'Dart seems in need of you, Doc.'

'On my way.'

Dr Field climbed the ladders and went into the cabin where Lees-Rimington lay. He examined the Captain as he had done so many times before, pulling down the eyelids, taking the pulse. He listened to the breathing. He said, 'There's certainly no improvement yet.'

'No, sir. Sod the bloody war, sir.'

Field said sympathetically, 'That's how I feel too. But it's not just the war. This could have happened just the same in peacetime.'

'Aggravated by the war, sir. And by what I did to him. That most of all, I reckon.'

So did Field, but he didn't say so. He said, 'What you did was for the best in your view. Don't brood. You're doing all you can now, and you're doing fine. There's hope, you know.'

'*Really* hope, sir?'

'Yes, certainly. As I've said, it's a mild stroke, nothing severe. It's a question of nursing mainly, not much a doctor can do.'

Under PO Blaker and the Stoker PO the seamen and engine-room ratings had gone through the ship like a dose of salts,

123

armed with such rifles as they had seized and still carrying the bunk boards as additional weapons. The German crew had been rounded up and were now safely imprisoned in the messroom, with an armed sentry on the door. In the engine-room a Lieutenant(E) had taken over, deputizing for his dead Chief. Now the dials and gauges and the great spinning shafts were being tended by British stokers and ERAs. Blaker acted as boatswain and detailed the seaman ratings for their watches and other duties. As the *Bottrop* steamed on, still under her original German ensign, Cameron called a confer-ence of the remaining officers and petty officers. This took place in the wheelhouse, covered against the wind and spray. Already Cameron had identified the Germans' intended rendezvous with the *Talca*: this was midway between Sal-vador in Brazil and Lobito in Angola – around four hundred miles north-west of St Helena.

'Four days,' he said. 'A little under. The weather's cutting our speed at the moment. If it improves ahead, we may make better time.' He tapped a pencil on the chart, where the rendezvous position had been neatly ringed by Schmidt with a time and date pencilled in alongside it. 'That checks with the Germans' intentions, near enough.'

Harvey asked, 'What exactly do you mean to do?'

'Make the rendezvous with the German ensign flying . . . no British uniforms to be seen, of course. When we're nicely within range, we open with the four-inch guns.'

'What's the *Talca* got, do you know?'

'Yes. The details are noted here.' Cameron held up a German ship-recognition book. 'Four 5.9-inch, one 60mm, one twin 37mm, four 20mms. Two 21-inch torpedo tubes.'

PO Blaker gave a whistle. 'Some opposition, sir!'

'Yes. But we're obviously going to get the first shot. We just have to get it in the right place, that's all. She won't have any armour plate. We have to get her magazines before she puts a shell into this tub's cargo holds. I reckon it's fifty-fifty.'

'I reckon it's suicide,' Harvey said. 'Look, we've got control, we've captured a Jerry ship and we can take her into a British port. Why not settle for that?'

Cameron said, 'The *Talca*'s a continuing threat to our shipping, Sub, that's why not. She's more valuable to the Germans than the old *Bottrop* – and her destruction's more valuable to us.' He turned to Blaker. 'Detail some guns' crews, please, PO. We have enough gunnery rates, haven't we?'

'Yes, sir, we'll manage,' Blaker said.

'Good. We'll exercise action till they know the guns inside out and can fire in seconds.'

Blaker went off to sort out the gunnery rates. Amongst the *Northumberland*'s survivors were two petty officers with the non-substantive rate of director layer and three leading seamen qualified as gunlayers; another had the rate of captain of the gun first class; and there were enough seamen gunners to pick and choose the best four-inch crews from. With the assistance of PO Maginess, one of the director layers, Blaker picked the action crews and detailed them for the port and starboard guns, housed behind hinged flaps in the side plating a little abaft the fore holds. The exercises began immediately: speed in getting the concealing flaps down and the guns in action would be all-important. The shells would have to go flinging across the gap the moment the flaps were down so as to exploit the element of surprise to the full.

'Surprise,' Blaker said, 'is about all we've got when you come to think of it.' He said this not to the assembled guns' crews but in an aside to PO Maginess. 'If you ask me, Mac, Mr Cameron's biting off more than he can chew. Still, there it is. Orders is orders. Do your best to knock the crews into shape.'

He went off, leaving the work-out to the gunners. Gunnery wasn't his line; he was a salt horse, a seaman pure and simple, though as a youngster he'd qualified as a seaman torpedoman just so he could put the badge up and get a pittance more pay for it. You needed to have something to put on your arm ... Blaker looked out at the frothing sea, at the spume tearing from the wave-tops along the wind. Dirty: and the guns' crews were going to get a wetting when the flaps went down and the sea drove in over them.

Dart divided his time between looking after Lees-Rimington and seeing to the officers. He was the only steward among the survivors and the officers had enough to do looking after the ship. He brought blankets up from the German officers' cabins; Cameron and Harvey were dossing down in the chart-room, handy for the bridge, and they were taking watch and watch, four on and four off. The two remaining engineer officers and a number of the chief and petty officers used the after cabins, which were right over the engine-room. Dart also saw to the meals, bringing the food from the galley where three cooks from the *Northumberland* did the best they could with unimaginative Hun food. Sausages, mainly. Big black ones. At least they sustained life which was the most import-ant thing. Dart had a job with the skipper, though; it was no use feeding him sausages, about all he could take was liquids. Tinned milk, water, soup. The soup was nourishing. Dart made him get as much down as possible. Dart was beginning to think the skipper was just a little better, not much certainly, but there was some movement coming back into his left side. He could flex his fingers and that must be a good sign, but he still couldn't get his words out.

Dr Field was cautious about it when he came to see how things were going. 'It's certainly not a *bad* sign,' he said. 'If it goes on that way ... well, we'll have to see, won't we?'

'Yes, sir,' Dart said. When the doctor had gone, he reflected that doctors never gave anything away, never committed themselves if they could help it. Perhaps it was natural: you could never be sure of anything in this life. If Dart had thought, before the war, that he would ever be in one Jerry ship in hot pursuit of another, with a load of Huns and a sod from the Gestapo locked in the fo'c'sle, he would have decided he was going, like Harpic, clean round the bend. But that doctor: Dart had a shrewd idea he didn't want to denigrate his own diagnosis ... just because he'd said the

126

skipper hadn't shown an improvement earlier, then the skipper was stuck with it, whether or no.

Dart found that a comforting thought and went about his work humming a happy tune.

Williams, the Leading Telegraphist, came to the bridge. 'Mr Cameron, sir?'

'Yes?'

'Picked up a signal, sir. From the *Talca*, addressed *Bottrop*.'

'Well?'

Williams said, 'It's in cypher, sir. German cypher.'

'Bloody hell!'

'The decyphering tables are in the wireless office, sir. I've got my mate seeing what he can do, but I don't hold out much hope.'

Cameron frowned. He had made enquiries earlier about possible German speakers among the *Northumberland*'s survivors and had drawn a blank. In any case no one would have had any knowledge of the German cyphering tables. There were, however, two men aboard who would: Schmidt, and the *Bottrop*'s radio operator. Pressure could be applied if necessary; Cameron had an idea that in the case of Captain Schmidt sheer curiosity might do the trick. He stared out into the gathering night. This was something of a poser: the signal could be dynamite. A warning to Schmidt, perhaps, of British forces in the vicinity? But if enemy ships were about then surely the *Talca* wouldn't have broken radio silence? On the other hand, to break radio silence at all must mean a high degree of urgency in one direction or another. Captain Schmidt would certainly be all agog.

The worries of command increased. Cameron roused out the Sub to take over the watch and went below with the Leading Telegraphist to talk to Schmidt, aware that any translation the Master might offer would have to be treated with caution.

The curiosity angle worked. Schmidt said, 'I will decypher, yes.'

The message was handed to him with the decyphering tables. Schmidt was not a fast worker: cyphering and decyphering were normally the province of his radio operator and there was much frowning and muttering and chin pulling before the job was done. Schmidt had naturally written down the plain language version in German as he had decyphered each group. He looked up and said, 'So. There is the message, Lieutenant.'

'In English, please, Captain Schmidt.'

'No. That I shall not do.'

'I shall have to insist.'

'I will not do it.' Schmidt made as if to rip up the transcript; Cameron clamped a hand over it in time, and gestured to the Leading Telegraphist, who wrenched Schmidt's wrist sideways. The German glared speechlessly as Cameron put the message in his pocket. The Leading Telegraphist caught Cameron's eye.

He said, 'I reckon we may manage, sir. There's a German–English dictionary in the wireless office.'

It was a laborious business and the translation was a rough and ready one but it sufficed: Cameron made out that the *Talca* had expended most of her ammunition in sinking a number of British vessels and replenishment was a matter of urgency. A new rendezvous was indicated in a position two hundred and fifty miles south of the original one. The *Talca* indicated that the bad weather had passed through her position and conditions were favourable. Schmidt was to be ready to transfer his cargo immediately on meeting.

Thoughtfully, Cameron went back to the bridge and resumed the watch. He felt it safer not to acknowledge the signal: neither he nor the Leading Telegraphist had any knowledge of German procedures. The Captain of the *Talca* might or might not be expecting an acknowledgement but was unlikely in Cameron's view to be particularly worried if he didn't get one. Schmidt could be considered reluctant to break his own wireless silence. Cameron felt the weight of the wind as it tugged at his clothing; full darkness had come down now, and visibility was virtually nil. After a while he became aware that there was some difference in the feel of the ship. She was handling curiously, seemed sluggish, and the sea was shifting on to her bow. Cameron was about to go into the wheelhouse for a check on the compass heading when there was a shout from the helmsman.

'Ship's not answering the helm, sir!'

12

'WHAT the bloody hell's up with it, Hutton?'

Able-Seaman Hutton shrugged. 'No idea in the world, sir. Unless the telemotor gear's on the blink. Must be that. She's not jammed, just moving free and sod all happening.'

Cameron ran for the engine-room voice-pipe. He called the Engineer Officer of the Watch. 'Helm's not answering, could be the telemotor. It's an emergency. Can you get some hands to check?'

'Right away.'

Cameron rammed the cover back and sent the bridge messenger for PO Blaker. Blaker was already on his way: he'd felt the movement of the ship, which was now heeling badly over to port as the waves pounded. As Blaker reached the bridge Cameron shouted, 'Emergency steering, Blaker. Have the after steering position manned at once.'

'Aye, aye, sir!' Blaker turned away and slid down the ladder. Cameron heard his voice, shouting for all hands on deck. Now the ship was coming broadside to the racing seas, lying farther and farther over to port as the waves punched and broke against her lifted starboard side. There was a frightening drumming sound, coming from God knew where, and then a surging heave of noise as something broke loose below decks. The cargo, the shells and explosives that filled the *Bottrop*'s holds? Cameron sent up a prayer. If there was anything very volatile in the cargo, a hammering such as that noise had indicated could be lethal.

Over she went, over and over until the port rails were practically in the water.

There was more noise. Terrifying noise, above the shriek of the wind.

The voice-pipe from the Master's cabin shrilled. Schmidt's voice said, 'My ship. What are you doing with her? I wish to come to the bridge.'

'All right, Captain.' Cameron sent the messenger below to tell the sentry to let Schmidt out of his cabin. Inside sixty seconds Schmidt was up there, swearing German oaths. Cameron said, 'It's the steering. The telemotor.'

'Never has it gone wrong before!'

'It has now.' Cameron was having to shout; the wind was increasing. 'I think the cargo's shifted, too—'

'So do I!'

'What's the most volatile element you're carrying?'

Schmidt said, 'Fulminate of mercury, amatol detonators . . . but they I think will not shift. They are very secure. That is, I hope they are.' He grabbed for support as the ship gave a heavy lurch, lifting for a moment back to starboard. Then she dropped to port again; there was a decidedly sluggish feel. Schmidt said, 'I think she is making some water somewhere, probably aft. You must send men to the after—'

'Sir!' This was Blaker, lurching across the bridge from the starboard ladder to bring bad news from aft. 'Secondary position's buggered too, sir. Won't answer. It's a right bloody lash-up, sir. Sodding Jerry ships . . .'

Schmidt said, 'Please. My crew can help now. Please. It is my ship. Everyone will do his best.'

Cameron met Blaker's eye. The situation was worsening fast. Blaker said, 'They may have the know-how, sir. At least they can follow the bloody instruction plates.' A moment later Cameron's mind was made up for him. The engine-room voice-pipe whistled. Cameron answered it, clinging to a stanchion to steady himself against the tilt of the wheelhouse deck. It was the Lieutenant(E): his ERAS and electrical artificers were stumped by the German telemotor gear. The *Bottrop*'s own engineers might be able to cope and it was to be presumed they would work to save their own lives.

131

Cameron said, 'All right. I'll get them along.' He replaced the voice-pipe cover and turned to Blaker who was standing by, looking anxiously towards the fore hatch covers. The sea was swilling half-way up them from time to time. 'Open up the messroom, Petty Officer Blaker. Bring the engineers out.'

'Aye, aye, sir.' Blaker made for the ladder, fast. Cameron called to him: short-handed they might be in an emergency situation, but the Germans were to be kept under guard. Captain Schmidt was given permission to go aft accompanied by the armed sentry.

Dart was having difficulty in Schmidt's spare cabin, where everything had shifted. Lees-Rimington had sprawled half out of the bunk before the steward had grappled him back in, doing he knew not what damage to the Captain in the process. Thereafter Lees-Rimington had been lashed down by means of a makeshift rope that Dart had fashioned from some shirts that had flown across the cabin when a chest of drawers had shed its load on the roll. He was more or less secure in a nightmare mess of shattered tooth-glasses, drawers, an inkwell and blotter from the desk and various odds and ends that had fallen from shelves attached to the bulkheads. Dart knelt on the deck of the cabin and did his best to hold the Captain steady, backing up the knotted shirts. After a while he was surprised to find that Lees-Rimington had lifted a hand and was grasping the metal grip secured to the bulkhead just above the bunk; it was the automatic response of a seaman when in danger of being thrown about in bad weather. *And the hand was the left one.* Dart uttered a silent prayer of thanksgiving. If this wasn't an improvement, then he didn't know what was. He wondered if speech had returned and he asked a question.

'All right, sir? Feeling better, are you, sir?'

There were indistinct sounds but no other response. The eyes were half-open but Dart didn't believe they were seeing anything. Apart from the apparently strong grip of the hand on the metal, the Captain seemed inert. Thanksgiving had

132

been premature. Dart remained in his kneeling position, listening to the howl of the wind, bracing his body and the Captain's against the appalling roll, which seemed to be all one way as though everything in the holds had shifted and was pinning the ship down in the trough of the raging seas.

'It can't be the telemotor,' Cameron said when Blaker came back to the bridge. 'If it was, it wouldn't affect the secondary steering, would it?'

'No, sir. Jammed rudder perhaps ... that was the feel in after steering. But if it was that, then the telemotor would have jammed up too, I reckon. And according to the helmsman, the wheel was moving freely enough in main steering.'

'Yes, that's true, but there could be a leak in the system, I suppose.'

The telemotor gear consisted, at any rate in British ships, of a steering telemotor in the wheelhouse, a motor telemotor geared to the rudder-head quadrant, and two small-diameter copper pipes connecting the two; and the system was filled with non-freezing liquid. By means of this incompressible liquid, an arrangement of piston-cylinders and levers was operated to open and shut the engine steam valves. If there was a leak or fracture in the copper pipes, then the wheel might, presumably, turn even against a jammed rudder, but Cameron was not sure of this. He asked, 'What about those German engineers?'

'I was just going to report, sir. They're working on it, under an armed rating apiece. There won't be any trouble, sir, not from that direction.'

'Good. In the meantime, I'm trying to steer with the port and starboard engines.'

'Not much luck by the feel of it,' Blaker said. He looked down at the fo'c'sle and fore well-deck. The list was shocking, but they might be all right if the ship didn't go any further over. There was that nasty drumming right through the plates as the seas smashed against their starboard side, rising up the ship to spill over and cascade down across the decks to foam

133

back into the water to port. They were entirely at the mercy of the waves and would remain broached-to until they could steer once again. Blaker sucked at his teeth: young Cameron was doing all he could but that wasn't much. He was tending the engines in a proper seamanlike manner, going astern on the starboard one and ahead on the port in an endeavour to push the bow to starboard and back into the wind and sea, but there was no noticeable effect. After a while Cameron realized that the attempt was futile and did what Blaker was about to advise him to do: he let the stern swing into the wind and then put both engines ahead, allowing the ship to run before the sea, accepting the risk of being pooped by the great surging breakers that followed up astern. After this the list improved a little and Cameron was able to maintain some sort of course by use of the engines. He had been steaming on the reciprocal of his intended northerly course for some fifteen minutes when one of the German engineers came to the bridge under escort of an able-seaman with a rifle.

'She will steer now,' he said in English.

During the investigation of the telemotor gear, the wheel had been immobilized. Now Cameron, going into the wheel-house, gave the order for the helmsman to try it out. He said, 'Starboard ten.'

'Starboard ten, sir.' The wheel went over. 'Ten of starboard wheel on, sir.'

'All right, Hutton?'

The seaman's face shone with sweat. 'All right, sir,' he said with relief. 'She's okay now, sir.'

'Good. I'm going to try to bring her round, back on course. Keep the wheel steady on starboard ten.'

'Aye, aye, sir, steady on starboard ten, sir.'

Cameron watched tensely; Blaker's face was strained as the bows began to swing, as the *Bottrop* fought to regain her course, butting to starboard into the wind and sea. Escorted, like the German engineer, Captain Schmidt came back to the wheelhouse, his face anxious. He didn't interfere; Cameron took this as an indication that he couldn't have done anything

134

better himself. Captive or no, his instinct was for the safety of his ship.

Round a little; then back again. Watching, Cameron asked the German engineer about the secondary steering position. 'There is jamming,' the man answered. 'Soon this also will be repaired.'

Cameron nodded, and caught Blaker's eye; the PO was looking sardonic. A lack of maintenance ... it just showed, the Jerries weren't as efficient as they liked to think they were. Alternative steering positions should be exercised at regular intervals. This one hadn't been. Meanwhile the ship was fighting hard; at last she began to gain some ground and Blaker stilled his misgivings. Again, if he'd been Cameron, he would still have run south for a while until the weather had moderated enough to make the turn without risk, but on the other hand he understood Cameron's desire to make the rendezvous on time. It was important to get the *Talca* if at all possible. On the loose, the *Talca* could sink a lot of ships, kill a lot of British seamen. The officer was right: he was proving it now. The *Bottrop* was making it – making heavy weather but coming round, inch by inch, to a safe bearing. There was a heavy impact of water on the bow still, but she was riding easier. It was going to be all right; Blaker let out a long, pent-up breath and realized that in spite of the dank cold he was soaked with sweat beneath his oilskin. It had been touch and go; it would not have been funny, to have been overrun by a sea. Many a ship had foundered under similar conditions. Down here in the South Atlantic, and round the other side of the Cape in the Indian Ocean too, queer things had happened from time to time and big ships had vanished without trace. As Blaker remarked to Maginess after he'd left the bridge, young Cameron knew something about ship-handling, seemed to have an instinctive awareness of just how far he could go.

By next morning the weather had moderated. The wind had gone, so had the spray. The seas were restless still and would remain so until they were further north. A swell had been left behind, but the motion was not too bad and it would be possible to carry out essential work below in the holds. The ship had a continuing heavy list to port, indicating a shifted cargo. Cameron sent down for PO Blaker.

He said, 'We can get the hatch covers off her now, I think.'

'Yes, sir ... there's no water coming aboard, it's true.'

'You sound doubtful.'

Blaker pulled at a lobe of his ear. 'Well, sir. There is something.'

'Go on.' Cameron was watching out ahead through a pair of German binoculars. There was nothing in sight. 'Feel free to speak!'

'Yes, sir. It's the hands. They're not trained in cargo stowage, sir. None of us are.'

'We can learn.'

Blaker clicked his tongue. 'Not with explosives, sir. Too bloody chancy! Why not leave it, sir?'

'Because that's too chancy, too. We're not going to have fair weather all the way. And there's another thing: with the trim gone, the four-inch guns can't bear.'

'The *Talca*, sir?'

'Yes, the *Talca* and anything else we might meet.' Cameron brought his binoculars down. 'We've got to right her, PO. We just have to. But I take your point about inexpert cargo handling. We could even go further over to port if we're not fully on the ball – which of course we're not and can't be. You realize what I'm getting at?'

Blaker nodded. 'The Jerries?'

'Yes. It's all we can do. That's a risk, too – I know that. I believe it has to be faced. As it is, we're useless and dangerous. We have plenty of hands to watch the crew in the holds.'

'Not to shoot at the buggers, sir, if they give trouble. Not in what's virtually a magazine.'

'I realize that! But they know they'll be dealt with the moment they show above the hatch ... and we'll have a hostage. Two hostages – Captain Schmidt and the Gestapo man, Leber. I've a feeling Leber won't countenance anything at all that might put his own skin in jeopardy!'

'Maybe not, sir.' Blaker paused. 'Why not just jettison the bloody cargo, sir, and—'

'No. That way, she'll ride suspiciously light. It'd be spotted at once from the *Talca*. We just have to re-stow.'

Blaker was doubtful still: it didn't seem sensible, to let the Jerries out. Last night – well, that had worked, it was true, and the Jerry black gang had done the job on the telemotor and the secondary steering, but that was a case of just a few men, not all the lousy bleeders. This was giving them far too much rope in Blaker's view; but the officer had made up his mind and that was that. Blaker asked, 'Do you want the lot up, sir?'

'No. Just the Second Officer and the seamen.' It was the Chief Officer who was normally responsible for cargo stowage and trim, but the Chief Officer was dead. 'And Leber. That's all. See to it, please, Petty Officer Blaker.'

'Aye, aye, sir.'

'And detail all our available ratings to muster at the hatches. Those without rifles can man the derricks under the direction of the German boatswain, that'll release all the ship's deck crew for re-stowing. I'd like you to have a roving commission ... take charge of security. All right?'

'All right, sir. And the Gestapo bloke?'

Cameron said, 'I'll have him up here, under guard. And Captain Schmidt.'

Blaker saluted and turned away. He went down the ladder fast. The sooner this lot was over and done with, the better he'd like it. The best place for Nazis, live ones, was locked up. To begin with, he didn't trust that Schmidt an inch; there had been crocodile tears since, but the shooting up of the boats and Carley floats had been Satan's work. Blaker would never forgive that. He got hold of a leading seaman and told him off to detail hands to open up the fo'c'sle messroom.'

'Tell 'em to watch it,' he said. 'Seamen, Second Officer and Leber only, and no funny business. They're to be escorted straight to the hatches and set to work getting the covers off.'

137

Blaker passed the rest of Cameron's orders and then took up his own station on the Master's deck immediately below the bridge, in a section of the deck where it narrowed in front of the square ports of the Master's accommodation. Passing the ports, Blaker glanced in. Schmidt was in his sleeping cabin, lying on the bunk, not asleep but reading. A few ports further along Blaker looked in again and saw Dart sitting in an easy chair, fast asleep. Lees-Rimington, on the bunk like Schmidt, looked bloody dead....

Blaker turned for'ard and leaned on the teak rail, keeping his eyes open on the door into the fo'c'sle. Upwards of a dozen armed British bluejackets were mustering at that door: the leading seaman had already gone into the alleyway with the unclipping party, the men who would stem any rush for freedom. Within the next minute they appeared, led by Oberleutnant Leber and the Second Officer. Leber was looking green: the atmosphere must have got him down, Blaker thought with pleasure. The Nazi tried to pull himself together when he saw the British ratings grinning at him from behind their rifles, rifles that had been German ones, but the result was unimpressive. Leber looked incongruous enough as it was, in his Gestapo tunic and badges and his once shiny jackboots. He didn't go with a merchant ship. He was clearly a very landbound landsman. Behind PO Blaker, Dart pushed the glass of the square port down and looked out.

'What's happening now, Blakey?' he asked.

Blaker told him. 'Very tricky, but I reckon we'll cope. How's the skipper, eh?'

'So-so. No real change.' Dart wasn't saying anything except to the Surgeon Lieutenant about that apparent improvement. No use raising false hopes, and in fact Dr Field hadn't seemed impressed; he'd just nodded and said that since the Captain still couldn't get his words out it was early days to be too hopeful. One ray of sunshine: the fact that Lees-Rimington had lasted as long as he had under adverse conditions was a miracle in itself. Dart said this much to Blaker.

'Let's hope the ruddy miracle's maintained, then,' Blaker

138

said. He said it as though he meant it. He'd been shaken by the skipper having put the Chief QM in the rattle over nothing, but the skipper's collapse so soon after had tended to put the injustice into perspective. A man did funny things when he was sick, things for which he couldn't perhaps be held responsible. In any case, the Chief QM had gone now, lost when the old *Northumberland* went down. His missus would never get to hear that he'd been due to go before the Captain, not that it would have mattered all that much if she had, not really ... skippers were funny people, largely, and wives had some understanding of the hazards attendant upon bad temper.

Blaker watched as Leber was marched forward; the jack-boots were poor stuff on a listed deck and the Gestapo man was having quite a job of it, slithering and sliding about and trying to climb sideways to avoid fetching up on the hatch coaming. At one moment he looked up and caught Blaker's eye; his face was sheer murder as Blaker grinned down at him. He knew he was to be the hostage, right enough. He also knew, most likely, how unpopular he was. His life could be on a shoestring now if one of the crew played up deliberately and the British were trigger-happy.

He vanished from Blaker's view as he was led into the superstructure and a few moments later the jackboots were heard clumping up the ladder to the bridge. Soon after this there were more footsteps, this time on the starboard ladder: Captain Schmidt. Blaker heard Cameron call down 'from the bridge to the leading hand in charge at the fore derrick. 'Right, Woods. Away you go, get the covers off.'

The work began.

From the north, the *Talca* dropped down towards the new rendezvous, making all possible speed in anticipation of meeting her supply ship. Her Captain was basking in much glory, as were all the ship's company: so many British vessels sent to the bottom, so many valuable British crews drowned or blown up by the German guns. The Führer was going to be extremely pleased and Captain von Eppler, a good Nazi but not one who subscribed to all the new notions, especially the one that said he should not use his von, expected honour and acclaim when he brought the victorious *Talca* safely into Brest.

But first there was more to be done – more to be sunk. There were still many fast ships sailing independently of the convoys, ships that carried troops, or oil fuel, or vital food-stuffs. These sinkings could not be achieved unless the *Talca*'s guns were fed, also her torpedo-tubes. The *Bottrop* was badly needed.

Why had her Master not acknowledged his signal? It would have been safe enough, as von Eppler said to his Executive Officer. 'There are no British ships – warships – in the whole South Atlantic other than the convoy escorts.'

'No known British ships—'

'Pouf! *I* know there are no British warships. That is good enough, Commander. The last one was the *Northumberland*. What happened to her? Sunk! This sea is an extension of the German Ocean.' Captain von Eppler threw out his chest and stalked up and down his bridge, bearded chin out-thrust and eyes shining. For a successful Captain, the world was a good place. Captain von Eppler thought for a moment about the crews of the ships he had sunk over the past few months. Poor fellows; they had had no chance ... von Eppler was about to formulate a message to be sent by wireless to the *Bottrop*, asking the Master to confirm his knowledge of the new rendezvous, when an officer came to the bridge and saluted.

'Yes, Handke?'

'A cypher from Brest, *Herr Kapitan*. An important one, addressed also to the *Bottrop*.'

Von Eppler stretched out his hand. 'Give it to me.' He read. He glanced quickly at his Executive Officer. He compressed his lips: this was unfortunately timed. A British cruiser was known to be in the South Atlantic; although well north of the *Talca*'s position she was believed to be heading south. She was a cruiser of the *Southampton* class, though her actual identity was uncertain. Von Eppler paced his bridge; heavy cruisers of the *Southampton* class carried twelve six-inch guns as their main armament, and they were capable of no less than thirty-two knots. Besides, they had armour plate, which the *Talca* had not. With the knowledge of this cruiser's presence to the northward, von Eppler decided that it would now be unwise to break wireless silence. In the absence of his orders to the contrary after receipt of the cypher from Brest, the *Bottrop* would naturally keep to the new rendezvous provided she had had his, von Eppler's, last signal. It had now to be assumed that she had.

The Commander, as von Eppler halted in his pacing, asked if there was to be any change in the orders.

'Change?' Von Eppler stared. 'No, there is no change. I shall keep to the rendezvous, and then remain in the southern part of the area. I shall not be deflected from my duty to the Führer by the movements of a British cruiser well to the north. *Heil Hitler!*'

He turned away irritably, mentally damning the Commander to hell fire. There had been a suspicion of a grin ... it was Satan's own idea of a joke that the signal should have come so soon after his confident assertion that there were no British warships in the South Atlantic ...

The message was received aboard the *Bottrop*; this time the Leading Telegraphist was able to crack it. He had seen Schmidt at work on that first occasion and some subsequent study of the German tables had made him reasonably proficient. Once again the German–English dictionary was brought into play and Cameron got the gist of the short message. There was some comfort in knowing that a British cruiser was moving south, but not a lot. The chances of her picking up the *Talca* or the *Bottrop* must be fairly remote. Cameron decided to stick to his plan and continue to close the rendezvous position. He should make that position in around seventy-two hours; in the meantime there was much work to be done by the German crew and their British overseers. To trim cargo at sea was never easy, according to Schmidt, who

141

remained on the bridge watching with a critical eye. The ship was not steady as she would be in port, and Cameron was aware that in port it was the stevedores not the crew who handled the cargo, though the ship's officers were responsible for the proper stowage and the trim of the ship.

With Schmidt, Cameron kept a close watch on the work in the fore hatch. Harvey was in charge aft and reported no difficulties. As the day wore on and the sun sank towards the horizon the *Bottrop* rode better: the list was very much reduced and the water had been pumped from her after sections. To work on in darkness would be dangerous, and the use of yardarm groups to give light would not be permissible: there just might be British submarines around, working out of Freetown, and the *Bottrop* would be a fine target. No submarine CO would surface to ask questions first. Cameron gave orders for the men to secure until morning, and for the German crew to be mustered back into the fo'c'sle.

Next day the work began again and by nightfall all was finished: there was no list now. Leaving Harvey in charge on the bridge, Cameron went down the ladder to take a look at the holds before the hatch covers were finally put back in place. He had a word with PO Blaker.

'A pretty fair effort,' he said. 'And no trouble with the Jerries!'

'That's right, sir, as good as gold they was.' Blaker removed his cap and scratched at his head, reflectively. 'Funny. The buggers worked as though it was still their own ship.'

'Professional pride?'

'Well, I dunno about that. Maybe, yes, sir. But it went beyond that, I reckon. There was a funny sort of confidence if that's the word. I don't know if they know something we don't, sir.'

Cameron shrugged. 'Such as what?'

'A German ship – other than the *Talca*, I mean – in the vicinity. That sort of thing. But I don't see how they could know. Not unless that Leber's in bloody Hitler's personal confidence and knows all the ship movements, and that's far

142

from bloody likely, eh?' Blaker laughed. 'I was probably just imagining things, sir. Not to worry!'

Cameron went back to the bridge. Harvey carried on the watch while Cameron snatched some sleep on the chartroom floor. Or tried to; although he was almost out on his feet, sleep did not come easily. He was in fact overtired, but had gone way beyond the boundaries; his mind was wakeful. Everything revolved, decisions, orders, projections for the future, the making of the rendezvous, the anxiety that there might be British merchant-ship crews aboard the raider when they met – all this churned and seemed to curdle. His duty was to sink the *Talca*, if he could, never mind who was aboard; but it was going to be a terrible action to have to take.

Sleep came at last, a very deep sleep. But it was interrupted. There was an insistent voice, an urgent voice. Cameron came back through the layers in response to it. It was Dart.

Dart said, 'It's the Captain, sir.'

'What about him?' Cameron sat up.

'He seems better, sir. Much better. The speech has come back a bit. He wants you, sir.' Dart paused. 'I told him you were in charge now, sir.'

'I'll be right down,' Cameron said. He went at once to the spare cabin. Lees-Rimington might be better, but he still looked a very sick man. His face was as white as the sheets on the bunk. One hand plucked nervously in the air, plucked at nothing. Dr Field was beside his patient.

'Cameron ...' The voice came out very slurred, and weak, as it had been at the start.

'Yes, sir?'

'I ... am unwell.' It was hard to pick up the words. 'The doctor ... on the ... sick list.'

'Yes, sir.'

'My steward ... tells me ... you're in command.' The voice went on, but Cameron couldn't pick up the sense. Dart interpreted.

Dart said, 'He wants you to give him all the facts, sir.'

Cameron nodded. He said, 'All executive officers senior to

143

me are dead, sir. I'm in control of the ship – the *Bottrop*, under the German flag.' As concisely as possible he gave Lees-Rimington a summary of the situation to date and of what he intended doing.

'The *Talca*,' Lees-Rimington said quite distinctly. There was a long pause, during which Dr Field gave Cameron a warning look that said the Captain shouldn't be tired beyond his strength. Then Lees-Rimington went on. He said, 'Captain von Eppler ... commanding.'

'Yes, sir?' Once again, Cameron couldn't pick up the rest of it when Lees-Rimington continued. Dart came to the rescue again: the Captain was saying that von Eppler was a nasty piece of work and should be sunk.

Cameron asked, 'You know him, sir?'

'By reputation. Must ... must be ... sunk.'

There was another long pause; Cameron ended it by saying, 'I shall do my best, sir. My chief worry's to do with any British prisoners aboard the *Talca*. When I open fire—'

'An ... an unnecessary worry. Von Eppler ... never taken ... prisoners.' Cameron listened closely and could just about pick it up this time. 'Leaves ... them to the boats, if there are ... boats. If not ... they drown. I shall ... have no ... no compunction in opening fire.'

Cameron was startled. 'You, sir?'

'I ... am resuming ... the command. I ... wish to be taken ... to the bridge.'

Beside him, Field said quietly, 'I'm afraid that's impossible, sir.'

'On ... on the ... contrary. I have given ... an order.'

'You're a sick man, sir. I can't allow—'

'Indigestion ... and weakness. No ... nothing more. You are ... not to mention ul ... ul ... ulcers to me again.'

'Not ulcers this time, sir. Something rather more serious. You've had a minor stroke, sir.'

'Nonsense, nothing ... of the sort. Now will someone ... kindly obey ... my orders and assist me ... to the ... bridge?'

Dart came forward, looking briefly at Cameron and Dr

Field. He said, 'If that's what you want, sir, I'll give you a hand, course I will, sir.'

He bent and put his arms around the Captain, his face full of concern.

'Leave him, Dart,' Field said quietly.

'It's what he wants, sir.'

'I said, leave him. That's an order. It won't help, to shift him.'

Lees-Rimington said, 'Leave my steward alone.' He said it sharply, less slurred than before. The Surgeon Lieutenant started to object again but changed his mind when he caught Dart's eye: that eye said something that was in fact close enough to the truth: if the Captain wanted to die on the bridge, why shouldn't he die there as much as anywhere else? Besides, like all stroke cases he was made worse by frustration – Field knew that much for sure. Perhaps it was a doctor's duty to interfere, to disregard a wrong order and to ensure that his patient had the best chance of living; but perhaps – in the circumstances – it was not. Field watched without further interference as Dart and Cameron carried the Captain to the bridge. A chair was brought up from the Master's accommodation and placed in the wheelhouse where there was a good view ahead and where Lees-Rimington would be under cover from the weather. The Captain sat and stared out at the ocean swell. There seemed to be no blood in his face at all, none in his hands. He was like a ghost, paper-white. There was a moon now, and stars; their light made Lees-Rimington look worse than the electric light in the cabin below had done.

Lees-Rimington turned his head and looked at Dart. 'You're a ... good fellow,' he said.

Dart didn't respond; he seemed on the verge of tears. The Captain glanced at Harvey, then looked ahead again. Suddenly he said, 'Flitting shadows.'

Uneasily Cameron said, 'Sir?'

'In the ... well-deck. Men, Cameron.'

Cameron looked down: he saw some half-a-dozen figures moving from below the break of the fo'c'sle. His heart gave a lurch: an escape from the messroom. He shouted a warning to the men in the wheelhouse and moved for the voice-pipe to the engine-room. 'Bridge,' he said. 'Stand by for trouble. The Germans have broken out.' He slammed back the voice-pipe cover, and turned towards Lees-Rimington. Then he saw a shadow moving from the head of the starboard ladder, coming fast for the wheelhouse door.

It was Leber.

Leber had a rifle in his hands, aimed inwards. He said, 'Do not move, Lieutenant.'

13

LEBER came forward slowly now, his eyes glittering. He was like a snake, beady-eyed, head weaving about as though ready to strike. Plegmatically, the able-seaman at the wheel continued to hold the ship on course. Dart moved protectively towards Lees-Rimington. Leber's rifle fired; Dart jumped and gave a yell. The bullet had grazed his sleeve, and had gone on to shatter a pane of glass screen. Fragments tinkled down.

'A warning,' Leber said. Lees-Rimington was motionless, one arm outstretched and gripping the sill running below the forward screen, holding himself steady. Leber went on, grinning now, 'You British are so stupid – such fools! Beneath the table in the messroom, under the corticene, there is a hatch leading below to the paint store. When you were shut in there we put a guard on the paint store, just in case, but you did not know of this. We waited until the dark, then we used this route, by-passing the British guard. The ship is in our hands again and you will do as you are told. For a start, Lieutenant, you will hand over the wheel.'

Cameron laughed. 'To you, Leber?'

'Not to me, no. In a moment I shall be joined by some seamen, German seamen.'

'Then we'd better wait, hadn't we?'

Leber gave no answer. A shot came from somewhere below the bridge, followed by another shot; then on its heels a scream. Leber grinned again and said, 'You see?' He. remained in the starboard-side doorway, covering them all, watching intently for any further movement. Cameron believed that, one warning having been given, the next shot would be aimed to kill. He glanced towards Lees-Rimington, who had neither uttered nor moved but was sitting rigidly on his chair. Then Cameron saw someone moving in from the head of the starboard ladder, clear in the moonlight. A German seaman, coming to take the wheel?

But it wasn't.

A moment later, as the figure advanced stealthily, Cameron recognized Blaker. What he himself had to do now was clear: hold Leber's attention riveted. He asked, 'Why didn't you attack during the re-stowing of the cargo, Leber?'

Leber laughed. 'We did not need to take the risk, since we had our way out when we could catch you napping.'

'It was all nicely planned, wasn't it, Leber?'

'Yes. We are Germans. *Heil Hitler!*'

Blaker was not far off now, moving like a cat. Suddenly Lees-Rimington came to life. He said quite distinctly, 'I shall not have those words uttered aboard my ship. Hitler is the enemy.'

Leber lifted his rifle. 'You are an old fool,' he said. 'The ship is German.' His finger was round the trigger of his rifle when Blaker got him. Blaker brought something heavy down on his head. The rifle went off and another window of the glass screen was shattered. Leber staggered, almost fell, but regained his balance and swung his rifle towards Blaker, who went forward in a flying tackle beneath the rifle barrel. Cameron moved in but was sent down hard by a wild swing of the German's rifle. As Leber tried to take aim, Blaker laid hold of the rifle and twisted it up, wrenching it from the Gestapo man's grip. Leber decided not to wait for it to be used against him; he ran full belt for the ladder and went down without touching anything. Cameron and Blaker ran behind him, saw him pick himself up and scuttle for safety like a rabbit.

'Yellow-belly,' Blaker said. 'You all right, sir?'

Cameron nodded. 'I'll survive. What's the situation below?'

'I don't know in detail, sir, but the buggers have got the off-watch men in the after messroom - took 'em sleeping and there's a strong guard on the door. They took the fore messroom sentry as well, before they—'

'That's about the whole lot, then?'

'Except for us on the bridge, sir, yes. I don't know about the engine-room.'

'I'll find out,' Cameron said. He went back into the wheelhouse and called the engine-room. The Lieutenant(E) was still in control. It was a case of so far, so good: the Germans had by no means taken over the ship yet. The Lieutenant(E) was confident of being able to hold out in the engine-room and boiler-room: no one, he said, would get past the airlock. He had four rifles and that was all he needed. Cameron replaced the voice-pipe cover.

Lees-Rimington spoke again. He said, 'Well done, Cameron.'

'Thank you, sir—'

'Outline ... the situation.'

'Yes, sir.' Cameron reported. He added, 'We have control up here, sir, so—'

'Yes. Bridge and engine-room. We shall ... consider ourselves under siege. We shall not give in.'

'No, sir.'

'And we shall ... sink the *Talca*,' Lees-Rimington said.

There seemed to be no response to that. One didn't contradict Post Captains of His Majesty's Fleet, but Cameron was left to wonder how they were to fire the four-inch guns with the crews under guard aft – as he had just told Lees-Rimington.

Dawn came in brilliant colours and the sea became flatter; there was little wind now, just enough to ruffle the blue water. The *Bottrop* steamed on under British control. Cameron, with Harvey and Blaker, kept the watch against any German attack whilst Lees-Rimington conned the ship. In fact he conned with his eyes largely closed; but the course was

149

already set for the rendezvous and could safely be left to the helmsman. Cameron had brought out the original firearms taken from the committal firing-party and kept in the chart-room: two revolvers and eight rifles, plus ammunition. They should be able to repel any attack mounted via the ladders. Constant communication with the engine-room showed that all was well down there. Matters were reasonably satisfactory for the time being but the showdown would come when they met the *Talca*; Cameron failed to see how they could survive that and still steam on for a British port. Lees-Rimington was not communicative on the point and each time Cameron made an attempt to obtain advance orders he was forestalled by either the Surgeon Lieutenant or Dart.

'He won't respond to pressure,' Field said out of the Captain's hearing. 'And he must not be worried.'

'He's got to be worried!'

'Why not carry on as if he weren't there? You managed all right before. Can't it continue that way?'

Cameron said, 'It looks as though it'll have to. I suppose I can rely on him giving tongue if things don't go as he intends ... but what *does* he intend, for God's sake?'

Field shrugged. 'I've no more idea than you have.'

'How is he, d'you think? Medically?'

'He's a bit of a miracle if you ask me.'

'Will he last?'

Field gave a tired smile. 'He's lasting, isn't he? I can't say more than that. But I don't believe he has a hope of making it back to UK now that he's refusing to take it easy. As far as that goes, I don't suppose any of us have.'

It was a strange experience, a strange existence in the solitariness of the bridge and wheelhouse. During the forenoon as they steamed on for the rendezvous position a man was seen briefly in the alleyway door beneath the break of the fo'c'sle, the sun glinting dully on metal. A rifle cracked as Cameron shouted all hands down into cover. A bullet zipped through one of the shattered panes and embedded itself in the wood of

150

the after bulkhead. PO Blaker was right on the ball: he fired back and a body toppled from the doorway and lay still, drooling blood. Soon after this the voice-pipe from the Master's quarters whined. Cameron answered it. It was Captain Schmidt.

'Why do you not surrender?' Schmidt asked.

'Why should we?' Cameron answered. 'So far, it's one up to us.'

'It is unnecessary, the killing. You cannot in the long run win,' Schmidt said, very reasonably in Cameron's view. A miracle could happen – such, perhaps, as the sight of a British battleship ahead! This was unlikely; and the cruiser that had been reported was well to the north. 'I ask you to surrender and let me resume the command. Then you will be well treated. If you do not, then Oberleutnant Leber may take stronger measures.'

'There will be ... no surrender,' Lees-Rimington said. He had heard Schmidt's robust tones coming up the voice-pipe. 'Tell ... the German that, Cameron.'

'Aye, aye, sir.' Cameron passed the unequivocal message down and the cover below was slammed in his ear. The day wore on with no change of watches. Cameron had organized some sort of relief system within his availability of men in the wheelhouse. He, Harvey and Blaker took a spell of one in three, only two being required at any one time to watch the port and starboard ladders; Dart and Field relieved the helmsman, finding no difficulty in steering a straight course through placid seas after a little instruction and practice. Only Lees-Rimington remained permanently on duty, cat-napping as before. He seemed to have some sort of inner fire, something that drove him on. Now and again his face was contorted with pain and he was as weak as a kitten, but he stuck it. There was an iron determination in him. There were no further attacks by the German crew; they probably saw no need. By now it must have become obvious to the Nazis that their ship was still on course for the rendezvous. The advent of the much more powerful *Talca*, even if some of them were to die, would

151

put paid to the British – so why stick their necks out now? That, Cameron believed, was how they were looking at it, otherwise it might have occurred to them, say, to interfere with the telemotor steering gear that they'd repaired....

Once again, night came down. There were seventeen hours left to the rendezvous. Cameron, on watch under cover by the port ladder, trying to keep his eyes skinned for signs of movement from all around, had the greatest trouble in holding the lids open at all. He was grateful when Dart, not on the wheel but unable to rest, came to talk to him, bending low in the lee of the steel bridge-coaming. To talk was the only way to keep awake ... and Dart was seeking comfort. Dart said, 'He can't last, sir. Not possibly,. he can't.'

'Don't lose hope.'

Dart shook his head. 'It's gone past hope, sir. It's as though he doesn't care any more about himself, only what he's got to do. What am I going to tell his missus, sir? I promised I'd take care of him.'

'She won't blame you.'

'I know that, sir, but it doesn't help—'

'You mustn't blame yourself either. It's the Captain's own decision, he's even disregarding the doctor.' Cameron strained his eyes through the moonlight. Each part of the superstructure seemed in his imagination to hold a German with a gun. 'I suppose you don't know what he's got in mind, do you?'

'No idea in the world, sir. It's all barmy if you ask me, and I don't mean any disrespect. I just don't see what he thinks he can do.' Dart was silent for a moment or two, then he said, 'Whatever it is, I want to be there with him, sir. He's been a good skipper to me. Got me out of a bit of trouble once, back in peacetime, when I was a leading officers' steward, him being the Commander. I got wrongly charged with nicking stores. If it hadn't been for him, I'd have ended up in jug. You don't forget that sort of thing.' Dart didn't add that there was something else he wouldn't forget, but Cameron knew well enough that the steward was blaming himself, had blamed himself all along, for his share in causing the Captain's tragic disability.

The German crew was keeping its collective head well down; the night passed, dawn came and went. The *Talca* should not be far ahead. The *Bottrop* sailed a peaceful sea, an empty sea beneath a clear blue sky. Like a zombie now, Lees-Rimington maintained his self-imposed watch, staring from a haggard face towards the north, not moving. He was obviously in pain again. The Surgeon Lieutenant would have liked to feed him fresh milk, which might have helped the ulcer he was still sure the Captain was suffering from; but there was no milk available now, and no other food either. No water; before long they must be starved out. The sun beat down, really scorching now as they moved into the tropics. The wheelhouse seemed close and airless; there was scarcely any wind at all, just a light breeze from astern which was negated by the headwind brought by their movement. The sea was a flat calm. The watch on the ladders was kept up. Still none of the crew showed anywhere on deck.

Harvey said, 'They're absolutely confident, aren't they?' His hands were shaking; he didn't like the situation at all.

Cameron nodded; it was just a question of time now. In the changed situation since the German break-out he would himself have altered course for a British or neutral port. Ascension Island would have been the best bet; then the Nazis would have shot their bolt – and yet, any alteration of course would have been noticed by the Jerries and then perhaps they might have buggered around with the telemotor. In any case when Cameron had suggested this to Lees-Rimington he had been met with a hard stare and the Captain's face had shown a touch of colour. The objective was still the *Talca* and, like Mad Carew in the Indian Army doggerel, nothing else would do. Lees-Rimington's mind could have become affected; if that was the case, then perhaps it was his, Cameron's, duty to disregard his orders and take over. That, however, was a very large step for a lieutenant; it would need medical backing, and that would be a big step for a newly-qualified doctor. The plain fact remained that Lees-Rimington had a duty to sink the *Talca* if he believed he could do so. To make any move to withdraw the *Bottrop* to safety could easily be misinterpreted by the Admiralty later on. But how in heaven's name was Lees-Rimington to sink the *Talca*?

It came in a sudden flash: *by ramming*!

Cameron's mind somersaulted. Was that in the Captain's mind?

He looked across at Lees-Rimington; then Schmidt came on the voice-pipe again.

'Why will your Captain not be sensible? At any moment we shall sight the *Talca* and then it is too late. Leber will revenge himself on all of you. If now you surrender to me, I will help. I will use my influence.'

Cameron said, 'It's no use, Captain Schmidt.'

'Tell to your Captain what I have said. Tell him that it is my desire to save bloodshed. Tell him all this, please.'

Cameron left the voice-pipe and went across to Lees-Rimington, whose eyes were closed again. He said, 'Captain, sir?'

'Yes, what ... is it?'

'Captain Schmidt, sir. He wishes to avoid bloodshed. He asks again for our surrender.'

'That is ... is an impertinence, Cameron. Tell him so. But wait a moment.' Lees-Rimington tried to lift the binoculars strung around his neck, but hadn't the strength to do so. 'There's a ... ship ahead. Identify it immediately.'

Cameron felt his guts react: Schmidt had just said, at any moment the *Talca* would be sighted. He could be spot on. Cameron brought up his own binoculars and studied the oncoming ship. It was still hull down: Lees-Rimington's eyesight was as keen as ever. Cameron said, 'I can't identify yet, sir.'

'I shall assume it's the *Talca*, Cameron.'

'A little early on the rendezvous time, sir, but near enough to be the *Talca*.'

'Yes. Orders ... orders for the engine-room.' The slurring was bad again, worsening. Cameron sought Dart's assistance in picking up Lees-Rimington's words. Dart, his eyes anxious, said that the Captain wanted the engine-room to start increasing to maximum revolutions in ten minutes' time, and when full speed had been attained the Lieutenant(E) was to stand by to evacuate all engine-room and boiler-room personnel the moment the executive order reached him from the bridge.

'Right,' Cameron said. He turned to the Captain. 'I understand, sir —'

Lees-Rimington broke in. Via Dart's interpretation he said that he estimated the two ships should meet in twenty minutes. In that time, the *Northumberland*'s ratings were to be released from the after messroom; the Captain believed, Dart said, that this would be easily done once his intentions became clear to the Nazis. When Dart had finished passing the orders, Lees-Rimington spoke again and, this time, his words were clear and they confirmed Cameron's suspicion.

He said, 'I intend to ram.'

The next five minutes brought the ship ahead close enough to be identified positively through binoculars as the *Talca* and within moments of this she began flashing what appeared to be her identification. Taking a rifle with him, Cameron, who had obtained the *Bottrop*'s signal letters from the chartroom, went at Lees-Rimington's order to the signalling projector mounted on monkey's-island on top of the wheelhouse and made the return identification. There was no interference from the Nazis, who were still lying low; they would know that the British were unable to use the four-inch guns and Leber would be seeing his time as about to come. As yet, the engine-room had not started coming up to full power and there was no indication of Lees-Rimington's intentions. When a further signal was made from the commerce raider, Dart was heard calling up the voice-pipe from the wheelhouse.

'Mr Cameron, sir. Captain says, no more signals. None of us speaks German anyway, 'e says, sir, and 'e understands

155

Captain Schmidt is already under orders to lie close to the *Talca* if the weather's suitable, which it is.'

'All right, thank you, understood.'

Cameron went fast down the ladder to the bridge just as the extra power came on the engines and the decks began to vibrate to the fast spin of the shafts. It was suicide, of course, but it could probably be brought off: the Captain of the *Talca* was expecting their approach alongside, if not at full speed; by the time he had realized the intent it might be too late for him. In the wheelhouse Lees-Rimington was staring down at the fore decks, slumped in his chair. As Cameron entered the Captain said, 'The crew . . . is coming . . . into the open now. I think they know now . . . because of the increased speed.'

Cameron looked through one of the shattered windows. There was a muster of the Nazi crew, plus Leber. A bullet sang past Cameron's head and he ducked. It smacked into the after bulkhead. Lees-Rimington said, 'Confirm my intentions, Cameron.'

Cameron inched upwards again and called, 'We are about to ram the *Talca*.'

Leber brought up a revolver but Cameron was the first to fire this time: the revolver spun away from Leber's hand and blood spurted. Now there was panic: everyone was only too well aware of the explosive cargo below hatches. Leber ran aft, shouting. The others crowded behind him, obviously heading for the boats. Lees-Rimington said, 'Now . . . the messroom . . . let the men out. And all . . . personnel out of . . . the engine-room.'

'Aye, aye, sir —'

'I . . . am abandoning ship.' The Captain's voice faded, then came back badly slurred. Cameron couldn't make out the words. Then Lees-Rimington said clearly, 'Dart.'

'Yessir.' Dart, looking pale and tense, faced Cameron. 'Captain says, sir, all bridge personnel will leave too. He's staying here, sir.'

'God, no! We'll take him to a boat —'

'No, sir.' Dart was adamant. 'Captain told me while you was

156

up top, sir, your duty's to release the 'ands from the messroom aft, sir, and then take charge of them in the water. He won't be an encumbrance, sir, and anyway, he'll be needed to steer the ship.'

'He'll never do it!'

Lees-Rimington turned his head. It seemed an effort. 'I shall,' he said. 'You are ... under my orders. You have ... eight minutes.' The eyes were bright now; the sick, haggard face was set.

Cameron was about to speak again but felt Dart's hand on his arm. Dart said, 'Don't you see, sir? He wants to do it. He's lost 'is ship, sir. He's RN – all the old ideas, Don't you bloody *understand*, sir?'

Cameron took a deep breath, shook his head in wonder, then saluted the Captain's back and turned away. Dart was probably right. The *Northumberland* ... in the RN tradition, the ship was the Captain, the Captain was the ship, one and indivisible. They both went down, if possible, together. It wouldn't be quite like that this time since the *Northumberland* had gone already, but near enough perhaps. Dart, who had saved the Captain when the cruiser sank, probably realized that, this time, he wasn't going to live long anyway. Cameron gestured to all the others – Dart himself, Harvey, Blaker, the Surgeon Lieutenant – a general indication that they were to carry out the order to leave the bridge and abandon ship. He called the engine-room and then, with Blaker, went fast down the ladder and along the upper deck to the after messroom, now unguarded. The clips were thrown off and the *Northumberland*'s ratings came out at the rush and, together with the engine-room staff, ran for the davits to get the boats lowered and away. One lifeboat was already at the end of the falls, manned by the German crew. As Cameron watched the boat was slipped – and slipped in an unseamanlike manner: it was not an easy manoeuvre with the ship steaming at full speed. The boat was dragged through the water by its after fall, and overturned, spilling its occupants. As more boats were lowered to the embarkation deck and were quickly filled,

Cameron looked for'ard towards the bridge. He was unable to see Lees-Rimington now but the *Bottrop* was headed straight as a die for the unarmoured side of the *Talca*.

There was very little time to go now.

At last, the German raider's officers had ticked over and the ship was turning away; but by this time she had reduced speed ready for the *Bottrop* to come up alongside and start discharging cargo, and she was answering her helm slowly and sluggishly. A moment later her guns came into action; as the *Bottrop*'s remaining lifeboats were slipped, this time successfully despite the high speed, the wind of the shells could be felt. Miraculously, the *Bottrop* remained unhit as she raced on.

The boats were left behind as the two vessels closed for the final act. Those boats were still pulling away when the *Bottrop* hit, smashing, so far as Cameron was able to estimate before the whole area erupted in smoke and flame, into the *Talca*'s starboard quarter. There was a crunch, a scream of tearing metal that could be heard clearly across the gap of water, and then a fractional pause, a kind of hesitation before cargo and magazines, torpedoes and guns all blew up together. Waves of heat swept across the men in the lifeboats, across other men who had jumped from the *Bottrop*'s decks and were now swimming for the boats' safety. The noise, the concussion was tremendous. Debris flew into the air, was suspended momentarily, then hailed down on the calm blue water. Another explosion followed, and another and another. It was some time before both ships had vanished. When they had gone there was a stench of burning and the sea was littered with woodwork and the contents of cabins and messrooms. Cameron stared at all that was left. Lees-Rimington had done what he'd wanted to; there was one German commerce raider and one German supply ship the less. Lees-Rimington hadn't a chance, even if he'd lived, of recovering sufficiently to have gone to sea again and there would have been no purpose left in his life. Now they had to think of themselves. Somewhere in the vicinity there was a British cruiser. The Leading

Telegraphist was in the boat astern of Cameron. Cameron called to him. 'Did you get a message away?'

'Yes, sir. The Captain sent the order by Petty Officer Steward Dart . . . I was to send a distress call in plain language, giving our position.'

Cameron nodded. 'Do you know if Dart got away?'

'I don't know, sir. He said he was going back to the bridge. Something about the Captain not being strong enough to take the wheel, sir.'

Cameron blew out a long breath. Very likely it had been Dart who had steered the *Bottrop* to her destruction, Dart who in effect had sunk the *Talca* – Dart who had disobeyed the order to abandon. Dart had wanted to be with the Captain right till the last; for all Cameron knew, Lees-Rimington could have collapsed again, died even, before the end. Dart had overheard the orders, knew his Captain's wishes, and all he'd had to do was aim the ship. That was all. Two very brave men had struck a blow for all British seamen who sailed the South Atlantic trade routes. And now Dart had no longer to fear telling the Captain's wife that he hadn't looked after her husband all that well.

Using the boat's compass, Cameron set his course ahead in what he hoped would prove to be the right direction for a pick-up by the British cruiser. The weather was kind now; they ought to be all right. If they were not picked up first, they could make Ascension Island. They pulled on through the scattered debris, British and German together. Cameron could see Captain Schmidt, and Leber; the Gestapo man was looking murderous at the thought of facing some of his own medicine: internment. Hitler wasn't going to be much use to him from now on.

Cameron was conscious of a curious sense of peace, in sharp contrast to all the happenings of the last few days. Peace, however spurious . . . there was going to be quite a lot of war yet.